ABOUT THE AUTHOR

Keith Cornwell's writing has been largely scientific non-fiction but latterly he has transgressed into fiction, albeit with a good dose of facts and fun involved. He studied both engineering and philosophy as an undergraduate student in London. Engineering led to his gainful employment as a researcher, teacher, Professor, Dean and such things in Edinburgh and latterly in the Middle East. Philosophy led to him to wondering what it is all about.

Keith Cornwell

TALES
from here and there

AUSTIN MACAULEY PUBLISHERS™
LONDON • CAMBRIDGE • NEW YORK • SHARJAH

Copyright © Keith Cornwell 2023

The right of Keith Cornwell to be identified as author of this work has been asserted in accordance with section 77 and 78 of the Copyright, Designs and Patents Act 1988.

All rights reserved. No part of this publication may be reproduced, stored in a retrieval system, or transmitted in any form or by any means, electronic, mechanical, photocopying, recording, or otherwise, without the prior permission of the publishers.

Any person who commits any unauthorised act in relation to this publication may be liable to criminal prosecution and civil claims for damages.

This is a work of fiction. Names, characters, businesses, places, events, locales, and incidents are either the products of the author's imagination or used in a fictitious manner. Any resemblance to actual persons, living or dead, or actual events is purely coincidental.

A CIP catalogue record for this title is available from the British Library.

ISBN 9781528969604 (Paperback)
ISBN 9781528977272 (ePub e-book)

www.austinmacauley.com

First Published 2023

Austin Macauley Publishers Ltd
1 Canada Square
Canary Wharf
London
E14 5AA

Introduction

This little book should not be read from the beginning but rather dipped into here and there as a distraction from whatever you should be doing. However, since you're now at the start, here is a very short summary.

Three dozen tales from here and there written over the last year or two are presented. Some are more or less true while others are flights of fancy. Some are from the past while others are set in the distant future. Some are from here in Scotland, written for my writing group, while some are located in lands far away. A handful are out there beyond the earth having being adapted from my book on Mars.

The tales can be read in less than ten minutes. Some feature a reflective point that may lead to contemplation for a few moments longer.

CONTENTS

One-Way Bungee Jump 9
Stamp of Approval 14
The Way it Works 18
Banter in the Mars Bar 22
Lockdown at the Zoo 27
Seeing the World 31
Good Samaritan 36
Butterfly Retribution 38
Rover Man 41
Messaging on Mars 45
Seeing Is Believing 49
London Smog 53
Coal Man 57
News Release 61
Rocket Power 65
Last Piece 68
Falling out of Grace 72
Food for Thought 76
Umbrella Thief 81
Senior Customer Care 84
Lost in Translation 88
Forgotten but not Gone 93
Rock of Ages 97
Final Adjustments 101
Abandoned Practice 105
Senorita de Mister 107

Sailing Club	111
Mum's Church	116
Running into Trouble	120
The Last Firework	126
Circumstantial Evidence	129
Village Kirk Hall	135
University Cuts	138
Bulb of Percussion	142
Family Tradition	146
Final Curtain	149

ACKNOWLEDGEMENTS

The author is grateful to the Tyne and Esk Writers Group of East Lothian, Scotland, for their general encouragement and to Sheila who, being partially sighted, had to endure the stories being read to her.

One-Way Bungee Jump

DANIEL DEVINE WAS approaching forty and he needed to do something new, something that nobody had done before. He had done all the usual athletic things like ski-jumping, water-skiing, rock climbing and even tight-rope-walking over the years and had earned himself the nickname 'Dan Dare' among his friends. Latterly he had tried high-fall bungee jumping, but then so had nearly everybody he met. He mentioned his ambition of finding something extreme and untried to his friends at the gym. One of them had told him to go and take a one-way bungee jump.

The others laughed but Dan, being serious-minded, started to analyse the idea. He reasoned that when you jump off the high platform you accelerate downwards but after a period as the bungee rope stretches you start to slow down, eventually stopping for a second before you start to accelerate upwards. At that second you are perfectly stationary and if the rope were exactly the right length you could have dropped down to be just on the ground. In theory you could then release the shackle and walk away. Great, the mechanics worked, so he Googled the idea and discovered one or two people had indeed done it before. Blast, that was always the case with his new ideas.

But then he read on and found it had only been achieved with short falls and usually where you held on with your hands: 'hand and release jumping' they called it. Maybe there was an opportunity here to make a high-dive jump and walk away and maybe, he thought with growing excitement, he could be the first to do it. He scanned all the commercial bungee jumping arenas in his local area and then all over Britain and even the whole world and spoke with them all, but none of them would entertain the idea, saying it was too risky. However, he was not called Dan Dare for nothing, so he continued the search to include unauthorised jump sites. Sure enough, there was a brand-new one recently established in Nigeria, deep in the Maasai Mara that responded to his email to say they would be happy to accommodate his special jump request. They added that he would still be expected to pay the full jump fee even if he was not returning back up.

Dan was delighted and he was nothing if not decisive. He booked his flights, gathered up his bags and was there within a couple of weeks. The little wooden jumping platform was high up in a tree which had grown out to overhang a deep valley full of small shrubs and bushes. The large Maasai tribesman in charge of the jump site assured him that it was all very safe as he had recently tried it himself. The depth to the valley floor was 62 metres, Dan was told, and it was designed for a 50-metre bungee drop at full extension. Dan explained that he wanted to perform a 60-metre drop, detach himself at rock bottom using a toggle latch he had designed and then drop the last couple of metres to land on the valley ground. When this was all agreed and paid in dollars, the jump manager set about extending the elastic rope while the tribesfolk entertained him for the night.

The next morning Dan felt decidedly drowsy and wondered what he had been drinking during the evening. However, on with the business: he and the jump manager duly climbed the rough ladder up the tree to the little platform. Now Dan was not one to shy away when the going gets rough, but he did have a moment of misgiving as he peered over the edge. He had, however, arranged for the event to be captured on video by one of the more competent tribesmen so there was no holding back.

'Are you sure about all aspects of this jump and that the latch will disengage, sir?' asked the Maasai jump manager.

'Of course,' said Dan, 'I've been bungee jumping before, you know, and wouldn't take unnecessary risks.'

Dan stood all geared up and ready to go, right on the edge of the platform. He continued to stand, so the manager gave him an almost imperceptible nudge and down he fell. The bungee length had been measured to perfection and as he slowed and slowed, Dan watched the ground came up towards him. At that point his iPhone fell out of his pocket and plunged down ahead of him into the undergrowth, but no matter. He successfully managed to release himself and fell the last metre or so face down onto the soft grass, just missing a spiky bush. He had done it: he was now the first to release himself from a high-dive bungee jump; he would be famous. He lay there for a moment in the long grass to absorb the pure joy of the success. He listened, but there were no cheers from the tribesmen assembled above, just an eerie silence. *Disappointing*, he thought, *but that's Maasai villagers for you.*

He arose a little shakingly and stood up; he must find his mobile. On looking around he noticed a glint in the sun of something bright by the base of a bush about 10 metres away. Next to it was another similar glint and, hang on, they seemed to move together. And, just in front of them was a very large nose and around them an enormous mane of straggly, matted, light-brown hair. Dan froze in petrifying shock. The instinctive message from his brain to run like hell was just not being received by his legs; they were quivering so much, his knees were knocking together.

The villagers had assured him that Leo and his pride never entered the valley. It was too near their grass-topped dwellings and lions are not overly interested in human beings. They were viewed as straggly and troublesome by the lions and over the centuries a jungle code of honour had developed where they each left one and other alone. Furthermore, the lions were not hungry, there being plenty of fat and lazy buffalos around. It was simply curiosity that had led them to explore the valley that day. Leo their leader was just minding his own business sitting by a bush feeling a little bored when out of nowhere one of these humans had effrontery to appear right next to him. Manna from heaven, he might have thought, had he known about manna and where heaven was. This needed assertive investigation and he crouched low ready to pounce.

At that moment the mobile rung. It was lying on the ground quite near Leo, so he went across to investigate that first. It shone and flashed in an aggressive fashion, so Leo crashed it with his paw. It still continued to ring so he smashed it again and again and eventually it stopped, this not being one of the standard Apple quality tests. Dan had recovered sufficiently to take advantage of the temporary distraction to back away and start climbing a nearby tree. He wasn't sure if lions could climb trees, but it was worth a shot. Leo then looked up at Dan, fixing him with a withering stare, then he opened his enormous mouth and let out an ear-shattering roar. Then he roared and roared again. Dan had an uncomfortable feeling he was roaring with laughter at him, a scrawny human being, quivering halfway up a tree. Finally, Leo gave the mobile one last dismissive crush with his enormous paw and wandered off.

After a time when all seemed safe, a couple of the villagers came down to escort a still shaking Dan back to the village. He could see them chatting in their own tongue among themselves and smirking. He knew that they were laughing at him and that the incident would enter Maasai folklore and be retold for ever. The tribesman commissioned to make the video had been so shocked that he failed to start the camera so there was no record of the jump. As Dan left the next day, he thought he heard, way across the shrubland of the Maasai Mara, a distant roaring and knew Leo was still laughing at him too.

Stamp of Approval

ALISTAIR HAD ALWAYS been fascinated by stamps ever since he had traded in five weeks of pocket money for an early penny red. He had seen it in the window of the newsagent's shop and fallen in love with it. To own something that had been cut out of a sheet of 144 such stamps with sharp scissors in some post office in the 1840s was the fulfilment of a dream. The light brown engraving of a young Queen Victoria with the minute plate numbers within the intricate lattice border fascinated him. It was duly mounted with a sticky hinge at the head of the Great Britain page in his album and remained alone in that prominent position until joined by a penny black with three wide margins. By then he was in senior school and worked a newspaper round each morning.

On leaving school and later university, he entered his chosen career of financial management. He applied the same determination to owning what he wanted and applied meticulous attention to everything he undertook. As a result, he was a multi-millionaire by the time he was forty, albeit something of a recluse because he was still totally obsessed with his stamps. In fact, that's not quite true because his success in the financial world had transformed this obsession into one about the value of the stamps rather than a love of the stamps themselves. He became well-known among the world's philatelists for owning some of the most sought-after stamps, especially those from the early days of the British Empire. The

Empire very much appealed to him, and exotic stamps symbolising the flamboyance and power of those times, especially if they were extremely valuable, represented items he must own.

Alistair well knew there were only a score or so of unique stamps and they seldom came on the market. They were usually owned by ultra-wealthy individuals or trusts who had no intention of selling because they constituted long-term assets and a hedge against inflation. Alistair felt it was a pity there were not more around as there definitely was a market need. There were quite a few stamps of which only two copies were known, and while these unique pairs were extremely rare, they did not command the values and attention of the few single unique stamps. It was this that led Alistair's obsession to take a rather sinister turn.

Through his philately club connections, he discovered that there were two Victorian stamps from an outpost of the British Commonwealth (discretion dictates it should not be identified) coming on the market from different collectors. They were priced at about fifty thousand pounds each, so he bought both of them. This was not the same as owning a unique one, but it at least meant he owned all the copies of this particular stamp. He then, over the next year or two, acquired several unique pairs and became quite well-known for owning these. They were very valuable so for security reasons he kept them locked in separate safes. Furthermore, as an added precaution in view of the millions of pounds involved in the total value of these stamps, the two safes were in separate locations, these being his house in London and his house in Edinburgh.

However, this was not enough for Alistair; he yearned for truly unique stamps with the only copy in the world in his ownership. Every time it arose in conversations at stamp conventions they would say, 'That's in Alistair's portfolios.' He soon realised that the only way of achieving this was for him to destroy one of each of the pairs. In the case of the Commonwealth pair mentioned, he estimated a truly unique one would be worth around a half a million pounds, giving him a healthy profit over the combined cost of the two. The trouble was that nobody would believe he had destroyed one of them.

The solution came to him one night after he had sat up very late admiring his collections and rearranging the stamps in his albums. He would have to have a public event in which he undertook the destruction of the sacrificial stamps so that the whole world would know what he had done. That would then mean he owned more unique stamps than anybody else, even if it did entail the destruction of perfectly good and rare stamps. He decided there was only one place for the public destruction: outside Stanley Gibbons, the famous stamp dealers in the Strand in London which, as it happened, was nearby his London mansion. He would invite famous philatelists to witness the occasion and of course the press, who as it happens again, were nearby in Fleet Street.

When the appointed day came the invited world-famous philatelists declined to attend the occasion – indeed, they were horrified and tried to deter him from this act of wanton sacrilege. The press either did not understand the significance of the occasion or did not consider it sufficiently newsworthy. In the event, he stood with only two onlookers, one being a representative of his bank whom he had insisted was present and the other a Russian oligarch acquaintance of Alistair's who was a stamp collector himself. However, undeterred by the poor turnout, he ceremoniously cut up seven valuable stamps, leaving him with the only remaining copies in his safe in Edinburgh.

It is good to have a happy ending, but unfortunately that was not the case here. A few days later his Edinburgh house burnt to the ground and the remaining stamps of each pair were frazzled to ash in spite of being stored in a reputably fireproof safe. As a result, the stamps involved no longer feature in the Stanley Gibbons catalogue as there are none left. The banker and the oligarch who had witnessed the event and accorded the destruction their stamp of approval each learnt a salutary lesson. Alistair himself, who was totally cut up about it all, became even more of a recluse.

The Way it Works

MOSUL ROSE EARLY, helped himself to a quick Arabic coffee and drove his gleaming white Range Rover out to the University buildings on the outskirts of Dubai. He had paid for both his son, Abdul, and his daughter, Aisha, to be educated at the Scottish University's new campus, but in his view the university had let him down badly.

He had complained previously to the university about them informing his son of his results after the first year of the engineering course rather than him, the father. It was true, his son was over 18, but it was he, the father, who was paying for this expensive education. His son was not of adult age in the Emirates until he was 21 and even then, they should have the courtesy to inform the patron who paid their exorbitant fees rather than the mere recipient of their services.

Now he had a more substantial complaint: his son Abdul had failed the first year. How could they allow that? As his father and patron, he had paid up front and it was up to them to ensure that Abdul was steered through to a pass. All in all, they had offered a sub-standard service and he was going to remind the new Head of Campus of his obligations.

As the new Head of Campus, I was lecturing to a third-year engineering class that morning. It was at a time when, however senior, all academics were expected to at least take some classes. Mosul was not best pleased at having to wait in the foyer in spite of my personal assistant supplying him coffee and some of those little Arabic sweetmeats. She introduced him as Mosul Mohamed bin Abdelfala and he flowed into my office in a gleaming white cotton dishdasha. I welcomed him:

'As-salaam alaykum, peace be upon you, and I trust you are keeping well.'

'Wa alaykum as-salaam. Yes, I am well, thank you, but not so peaceful this morning as my son, whom I entrusted to you to obtain his engineering degree, has apparently been failed by your university at the first hurdle.'

My assistant passed me an open file which reminded me that his son, Abdul was one of those who had failed the first year rather badly.

I rapidly perused the file while his father was continuing:

'… and I paid many dirhams to the university to have him educated to your exacting standards and I expect him to pass. When I buy a new car, I expect it to work. If it fails, then I expect it to be repaired and serviced until it is usable again. I don't expect to be told it has 'failed' and cannot be used. In the Emirates, that is deemed to be trading unfairly. Also, you should report directly to me as the contractor, not to the recipient of the service.'

Before he could go any further, I came in with:

'That's not the way education works. We are providing an educational service to your son, but it is he who must take on board that service, rather like a keen sportsman can benefit from the input of a good trainer.'

I was interrupted by my assistant who placed a second file in front of me.

'Mosul Abdelfala, I am reminded that you have a daughter, Aisha, here too, and she has passed her second year in

Business Studies with flying colours. In fact, she was our best student in that cohort.'

'Ah, that may be so,' he said, 'but it is my son who is my primary concern. I run a carpet manufacturing business and one day my son will partner me, so it is imperative that as a future head of the family he does not fail. I will be discredited by all my associates as well as my family if he were to fail.'

'I understand, but unfortunately the records show he failed very badly, indeed he failed every single subject. We cannot even allow him one or two resits under this condition. All we can do is to issue an attendance certificate which will at least mean he has something in writing.'

My assistant who was hovering at the door overheard and mouthed 'no,' shaking her head. I looked again at the file; at the end was a wee note to the effect that Abdul had not attended classes at all.

'I'm afraid I have to inform you that your son did not attend any of our classes after the first week and that apparently his tutor did email you about this. The tutor has noted that in his view Abdel was ill-suited to an engineering education.'

The ensuing pause was broken by Mosul saying quietly:

'I would be happy to pay any penalty your university wishes to impose on him.'

'Payment in lieu of performance is completely unacceptable,' I said sharply. 'That is the way it works in the West.'

He said nothing and just stared into the distance for a time and then admitted:

'I only have an email address to appear professional; I never actually use it.'

After a pause I said:

'May I commend you on the excellent progress of your

daughter. As I said, she is our star student, and we look forward to her obtaining a good degree.'

We shook hands and he left. I did not expect to see him again because I retired that summer and returned to the UK.

However, three years later, I was in Dubai for other reasons and found that the university graduation ceremony was occurring while I was there. For old times' sake and to meet a few friends I decided to attend. Who should I bump into but Mosul Abdelfala?

After formal greetings, I ventured:

'No doubt you are here for your daughter's graduation?'

'No, I am here for my son's graduation. Abdul repeated the whole year, attended every class under my watchful eye and then saw the course through to the end.'

'That's really great. And your daughter?'

'Aisha abandoned the course to marry Sheikh Mohammed bin Hafnah and is now his premier wife and business secretary. He accepted my carpet business as a dowry and Abdul and I are proud to be the executive directors of his new company.'

'That's the last thing I expected, but I am pleased for you,' I exclaimed.

'That's the way it works in the East,' he added with a smile.

Banter in the Mars Bar

(*Rejected for the December 2036 magazine* Mars Weekly *owing to persistent infringement of current Mars cultural and gender identity guidelines.*)

AFTER CHAT ABOUT UK football and the re-emergence of Rangers following their slump on the world scene in the early '20s, as John liked to remind his Scottish friend, they degenerated into moaning about the miserly beer allowance. To add insult to injury, it was dispensed directly into their plastic mugs from a steely robotic device known unofficially by Mars folk as Greta, owing to it being so unlike any Bavarian barmaid they'd ever seen. The conversation then drifted onto their work and people issues.

John was responsible for the bio-engineering research group in the Mars Colony and his Scottish friend, Rev Steve McKay, being the Mars Chaplain, was seen by the scientists as the first port of call for any people issues.

'I see you referred your bright young assistant to me as soon as she fell short of your work routine expectations,' said Steve with a quizzical smirk.

'Yes,' replied John. 'Several times she has been late at her workstation and once did not turn up at all. She is brilliant at her job but seems to suffer more than most from terrestrial nostalgia.'

'Don't we all?' said Steve. 'It is the little things of life that we had got used to on earth and hardly noticed but are now no longer there that constantly remind us we are in some ghostly post-terrestrial experience – on which point, have I lost it, or is that a fly on my glass?'

'It's sure a fly all right, Steve, but that doesn't mean you haven't lost it,' chided John. 'I heard the other day that somebody had seen one.'

'But that's terrible. All this talk about not seeding Mars with earth's microbes and the precautions we have to take and yet it's failed. Isn't everything meant to be biologically screened? – Surely flies would be noticed.'

'Apparently not,' said John. 'The eggs are less than one millimetre across. Do you know the female housefly only copulates once in her life (let's hope she enjoys it) and secretes the semen for subsequent egg fertilisation? She can lay hundreds of eggs every few days over her lifetime so that's why they're everywhere on Earth – there're bound to get transported with something.'

Steve was hardly listening as he was thrashing around trying to swat the fly with a plastic menu, but John admonished him. 'Just let it be, it's a small reminder of home and you need to preserve these links with life down there, even the flies.' He then continued, 'Talking about flies, I was once in a pub with an Englishman, a Welshman and a Scotsman…'

Steve gave an exaggerated sigh and muttered something about here we go….

'Three flies flew in the window, one landing on each of their three pints. The Englishman got a teaspoon, delicately eased it out and continued to drink. The Welshman waited for it to float to the centre and then, in a show of wild determination, flicked it out using his thumb and forefinger with such force it was impaled on the window pane. Your countryman, the Scotsman though, he just waited until the fly's attempts to swim subsided and it lay immobile on the surface. He then squeezed it out over the pint, wiped the residue off on his kilt and drained his pint.'

'Okay, okay,' said Steve. 'Actually, we call it fly fishing.' He then added, 'And did *you* hear about the two Scotsmen, two Welshmen, two Irishmen and two Englishmen who got stranded on a desert island. After three months the Scotsmen had made a whisky still and were selling it to the others; the Welshmen had started a choir, the Irishmen were still fighting on the beach but the Englishmen still hadn't spoken to each other as they'd not been introduced.'

John realised he was not going to win this line of banter and after a pause returned the conversation to flies. 'Isn't it amazing that flies' eggs can survive the journey here?'

'It's no more amazing than me surviving it,' said Steve.

John looked at Steve oddly. 'We've all survived that. What makes it so special for you?'

Steve took a considered sip of his beer. 'Well, physically it was not too bad, a bit cramped with 47 of us in a space not much larger than a double-decker bus. You eventually get used to all the minor frustrations, the hanging on to everything to stop it floating away, drinking through flimsy straws, pissing into plastic bags, constantly having to catch your screwdriver every time you do a repair job and so on. No: it was seeing the earth get smaller and smaller until after three months you saw it only occasionally and only then as a wee dot in the sky. That dot was my total existence, my total life up to the age of 37, and now it is nothing.'

John responded thoughtfully, 'Most of us spent so much time sorting out the petty annoyances of everyday living on the spacecraft that we had little time for philosophical thoughts like that. But I suppose that's part of your job and you have got to deal with it and have answers. I really don't envy your role as chaplain, but drink up and I'll get you another one before you become melancholy.'

'I thought we were only allowed a half-pint per day,' said Steve. 'That's the rule, isn't it? And I of all people must be seen to observe these ruddy rules,' he grinned.

'The rules are made by folk on the wee dot you mentioned just now so I should not fret about it. I'll tell you what: I'll order two for myself from that damn machine that calls itself a barmaid and then you can offer to drink one of them to avoid me sinking into the wanton sin of disobedience to our masters – that's what you folk are meant to do, isn't it?'

John had to override the voice-over warning on the dispensing machine in order to extract two more beers, one of which he placed in front of his friend. Steve said nothing for some time but after a while he made an admission that he had told nobody else.

'Since you ask,' he said, 'I had no trouble with lift-off but about an hour afterwards I found I was totally emotionally drained, feeling horribly alone and somehow disconnected. Basically, I suppose I was shit-scared – excuse the non-liturgical language, but I realised for the first time that I was dead. All the molecules and thoughts that make up *me* had left the Earth; I was no different to anybody who's dead. I was totally dead to them, but I knew I was still alive. Maybe that's a pre-amble of being dead in any form. I'm still thinking it all through.'

John was used to jollying his oddly pious friend along with rib-digging insults and targeted jokes but sensed this was not the right response at the moment. He was just about to say that it might be true for the molecules but not the thoughts which floated around forever like emails in the cloud when he was saved by Fiona. She joined them with no sense of interruption and asked why they were looking like two jerks planning a bank raid. John glanced at Steve with a 'maybe we'll continue this some other time' look and they gave Fiona, a lively personable girl in her late 20s working in the metallic materials lab, their full attention.

Lockdown at the Zoo

GAVIN LOVED HIS iPhone. It was his constant companion, the fount of all knowledge, the means of contact with his university friends. However, now that the lockdown was being cautiously lifted, he needed a dose of reality; there must be more to life than screens and electronic pulses. One sunny morning he noticed that Edinburgh Zoo was partially reopening and managed to obtain a visiting slot. After all, the zoo had always been locked down where the poor animals were concerned so he could at least empathise with them.

It was outside the monkey enclosure that the incident occurred. The little Capuchin monkeys are among the most intelligent and friendly and he was fascinated by a particularly lively one who looked in his direction when he called out 'Capuchin'. He tried to capture a good photo but the wire fencing was in the way and his grey hood kept falling forward. After several tries using both hands he managed to carefully manoeuvre his iPhone just inside the wire and was rewarded with an unrestricted shot. Suddenly, Capuchin jumped across from nowhere, snatched the iPhone and darted away into the distance clutching it gleefully. To Gavin's utter dismay he saw the monkey stabbing at the screen with his forefinger and squealing with delight as it lit up and strange coloured symbols appeared. Capuchin proceeded to show it to his friends who tried to snatch it from him, but he clung onto his new toy.

Gavin panicked and searched around with the vague idea of finding a zookeeper to help. There was nobody near except a lady visitor all bundled up in knitted jumpers in spite of the sun, who seemed mildly amused that this young hoody had unintentionally donated his mobile to the zoo. Did she not realise this was his life and all that he held most dear was being manhandled with alacrity by a monkey? He prayed that some miracle would occur as he watched helplessly.

Capuchin was now sitting on a branch examining the back of his prize and peering in puzzlement at his own reflection. He then gave Gavin a long quizzical look, pondered for a moment, swung across and handed Gavin back his precious iPad, even helping him angle it through the wire fence. Gavin was completely taken aback. As he stared into Capuchin's deep brown eyes something clicked into place. He saw a look of pure primeval kindness. He remained staring until the spell was broken by knitwear lady, who remarked as she walked off:

'That must have been meant to be, lad.'

Gavin was studying mathematical physics. He had learnt how the universe works; how we are all just assemblies of atoms with large gaps between them. The atoms all obey the laws of the universe, the same laws that determine the paths of the planets and galaxies and everything, but just on a different scale. Einstein and Hawking and their like had perfected a Theory of Everything which had seemed somewhat immodest until he realised these atoms and their constituent parts are indeed everything and there is nothing else left to find. We are all the natural consequence of these laws and subsequent evolution by natural selection. Yet that look of pure kindness, from way back down the evolutionary chain, had completely zonked him. Were the atoms not everything, after all? They said some kindness may be expected if it aids development of the species, but this did not account for the pure, unrequited kindness he had just witnessed. That must have come from somewhere else. It certainly did not evolve from a soup of chemicals swilling around billions of years ago. Was it *panspermia*, that germ of life there from the Big Bang that we have as yet failed to isolate, the humus that transforms the inorganic into life, the elusive spirit that the ancient mystics had called the love of God?

As lockdown eased, he pondered over this and discussed it with a friend who introduced him to one of Edinburgh's many evangelical churches. They welcomed him like a long-lost brother in spite of social distancing, so he cautiously went again the next week and the week after. However, it troubled him that the Church seemed to focus on events that occurred 2000 years before his iPhone and, worryingly, implied he was forever sinning and consequently destined for hell unless converted by them. He couldn't think of any dreadful sins he'd committed recently except for pilfering paper from the university printer and seriously breaching Government distancing guidelines one evening during the lockdown with the lovely Cynthia.

One Sunday evening an enthusiastic youth leader and his followers cornered him after a Service and asked him about his 'conversion'. He was not sure what to say but being put on the spot he went on to explain how he had experienced a sort of revelation from a monkey at the zoo. The leader seemed affronted by this disclosure and took it quite personally. Gavin was not invited again.

However, he also began to realise that the same kindness he'd experienced at the zoo actually seemed to be everywhere. At the beginning of the lockdown a guy two flats above, who had previously ignored him, chatted with him one morning and gave him some spare toilet rolls. A robust older lady in the adjacent flat gave him half a chicken-and-leek pie saying she'd made too much. The next day he fixed her window latch and was rewarded with half a rhubarb flan for his trouble. Maybe it had always been like this with folk but he had never noticed it before.

He kept chipping away at the intellectual problem of where all this pure kindness came from; he was, after all, a budding mathematician and scientist. He eventually concluded it was indeed everywhere in the universe, like the waves received by his beloved iPhone. You just needed a receptive mind to tune in and open up an arena of consciousness that seemed even more extensive and mystifying than the electronic one. Maybe this arena of individual kindness, which mitigated whatever disaster the physical world threw at us, was where this elusive God really resided.

Meanwhile, whenever times were hard, Gavin would visit the zoo and stare into the deep clear eyes of the animal kingdom.

Seeing the World

DAREN AND FATHER O'Brian were both on death row but for very different reasons. They were sitting alone in the little departure cubicle that had been constructed high up in the metal tower that supported the enormous gleaming starship atop the rocket that would soon blast off on its six-month journey to Mars.

Daren, 32, was prisoner 5738 on death row in Florida State Penitentiary. He had been there for 10 years, following the compulsive homicide of a violent brute who had attacked his girlfriend with a knife. Unfortunately for Daren, any potential sympathy was negated by the fact that he had blasted the brute with the full load from his new Ruger 10-shot revolver when one shot would have been sufficient; a complete over-kill, they said. His lawyer was still arguing for mitigating circumstances but like the other cases this took time – many years indeed – and he had meanwhile volunteered to be one of the early astronauts allocated a non-return passage to Mars.

Daren was just one of nearly 4000 USA inmates on death row. This number had risen steadily from 2500 in the early 2020s, and the Federal Government had recommended that States that still had the death penalty consider sending some of them on one-way missions to Mars. When first mooted, this idea had caused much public debate and soul-searching among the various ethical committees. However, it was pointed out that the UK had sent nearly 200,000 folk to Botany Bay in the past, including children who had merely stolen bread, so it must be okay. It was finally settled by a committee of the inmates themselves, who recommended that only those on death row who volunteered should be given this alternative to the lethal injection. In the event, the 'Death on Operation Mars' or DOOM programme was heavily oversubscribed, so they were short-listed with those committing particularly heinous crimes having priority over those deemed only marginally death-worthy. Using 10 bullets when one would do placed Daren high up the list and as a result he was selected to go on this last voyage.

On Mars the prisonauts, as they were called, were expected to labour on the construction of the vast domes being built for human habitation. This was exhausting work, cementing the joints between the concrete blocks that formed the shell of the domes. Both the blocks and the jointing cement were formed from the sandy regolith found in abundance on Mars, mixed with a minimum of water which was also present but in limited supply. The spacesuits were restrictive to movement and each shift was about three hours, by which time they wearily returned to their base: another dome completed previously. However, two shifts a day left plenty of time to relax, watch local TV, eat and socialise with colleagues in the completed domes. All in all, life was bearable for prisonauts in the short term even if the long term prospects were grim. But then, long-term prospects were grim on earth, particularly if you were on death row.

When first incarcerated and placed on death row, Daren had dreamt every day of the time when he could once again roam the open fields of home, but these dreams had faded over the years. Now it seemed the only freedom he could ever hope for was shuffling along the Martian sand in his spacesuit millions of miles from the world he loved. But enough about Daren, what about this priest sharing the little pod next to the starship?

Father O'Brian was the NASA Catholic Chaplain. In his youth he'd had dreams too; dreams of seeing the world and doing memorable things. But they were not to be and he'd ended as the Verger of St Mary's in a small town near Cape Canaveral in Florida with occasional duties as the local NASA Chaplain. These duties included offering sacramental blessings to those about to leave in spaceships to the Space Station and latterly to Mars. This now included some of those on death row, a government move which he did not condone.

However, a disaster had struck Father O'Brian a few weeks before when he had collapsed and been taken to the local hospital, there to discover he had an inoperable brain tumour. He was despatched from the hospital with no hope of survival and reeling from the shock. Now he felt that he too was on death row. Consequently, there was some empathy with poor Daren and on earlier visits they had developed a certain rapport, each discussing the dreams of their youth and lamenting their non-fulfilment. Daren enquired of Father O'Brian what he now planned to do during the next few months while he was still able. Father O'Brian was touched by his concern and revealed a secret: he had some considerable life savings, unusual for a priest, and after much soul-searching was intent on using them for a good cause or at least righting some injustice in the world. As a first step in this direction, he had withdrawn them from the bank in bundles of notes and currently had them all hidden in obscure pockets in the boot of his car. He explained to Daren that he was planning to distribute them as the spirit guided and they discussed at length how this could be done. An odd discussion, it may be thought, for a convict on death row to be having with a dying chaplain, but that is life.

The Federal authorities had proscribed a rigid routine for the final hours of a prisoner as he or she left the earth, not unlike the routine for an execution. It was a ceremonial occasion akin to the last rights and Father O'Brien was expected to follow this routine to the letter as part of his contract. Essentially the prisoner, already in his space-suit except for his darkened glass helmet, would be in the cubicle and ready to go. The chaplain would conduct a short service involving a reading from the Bible, or other religious book if not a Christian, and offer appropriate prayers for the condemned person.

On the day of lift-off, the two were together in private in the little departure cubicle on the tower. Daren was already encased in his space suit except for the darkened-glass space helmet by his side. Father O'Brian, now in his vestments and cassock, outlined the proscribed procedure. This involved reading from the Bible and prayers to the saints, followed by the chaplain placing the helmet over the inmate's head, locking it in place and sprinkling with holy water. The chaplain would then press a red button to open the door of the cubicle and exit, leaving the condemned inmate to be taken by the tower staff on the short walk across the bridge from the tower to the astronaut's pod high up in the spaceship.

Daren grimly nodded that he understood what was expected of him.

Precisely 45 minutes later, the starship above the massive booster blasted off from Cape Canaveral into the early morning haze without a hitch, like the many hundred or so rockets before. Precisely an hour after that, when the booster had long since been jettisoned back to earth and the air in the pod had stabilised, astronauts were allowed to remove their helmets for the first time and view the surroundings. But when the time came for the dark plastic helmet to be removed, it revealed not Daren but a rather ruffled Father O'Brian. He apprehensively viewed his surroundings and saw a small window looking out to space. And there it was: the whole Earth in all its glory. He watched mesmerised as the green and blue globe receded into the blackness of space and uttered a short prayer of thanksgiving that he had been spared to see the world and fulfil his teenage dream. He then began to wonder how Daren was getting on.

He need not have worried. Somebody reported they thought they had seen the chaplain in his cassock with his hood up, running with remarkable agility for a man of his age towards his car in the parking lot. It was later found abandoned in North Georgia with no contents of any kind in the boot. No sign of the driver was ever reported.

The Federal government were remarkably uninformative about prisoner 5738, stating that the information they had on him was highly classified and would not be released for 25 years. NASA quietly modified its procedures for chaplains offering the final rites. Nobody on earth knew what became of Daren but somebody on their way to Mars had an inkling.

Good Samaritan

LADY ANGELA HAD been feeling a little down, so she booked a short break at a boutique hotel situated within a small village in the heart of Shropshire. Sunday morning was dull and dreary but nevertheless she donned her Jaeger coat, grabbed her matching umbrella and set off down the lane for matins at the so-called *Church of the Good Samaritan*.

Walking back after the short service, she almost stumbled over a man lying at the side of the lane.

'What happened, are you hurt?' she enquired in alarm.

The man told her how he jumped out of the way of a passing car and tripped over the curb.

'Some hiker came by, peered at me and walked off. Then a priest, probably from that Church down there, passed by on the other side. I really need some help to get up, please.'

Lady Angela checked he was not seriously hurt and then helped him to his feet and onto the bench.

'Have you friends or family nearby? You've obviously had a nasty shock.'

'No Mam, I've no relations left. I used to manage well but now I'm sleeping rough.'

She felt sorry for him and helped him along the road to the nearby pub where he slumped into a corner seat. She asked the landlord to look after him and provide him with food and lodging for the night, paying him generously for the request.

She left the pub, but it started to rain which reminded

her that she had left her umbrella there. She went back and on entering heard the landlord say:

'I've put you in the same room as last Sunday, Bob.'

She was shocked and for a moment her blood boiled, but then she took a deep breath and calmed down. As she walked back to her hotel, the rain stopped, the sun shone through, and she felt happily uplifted. The vagabond and the pub landlord were also happy, which shows that, come what may, kindness leads to happiness all round.

Butterfly Retribution

ROBERT LOVED HIS butterflies. He kept them in wire cages in his well-appointed butterfly shed down the bottom of the garden. It was an ancient garage but had been transformed with an old sofa, a coffee machine and piles of magazines into a comfortable pad both for him and the butterflies. At night the butterflies would sleep under the leaves of the plants in the cages. One evening he had switched on a torch and shone the beam into their cage, taking a primitive delight as he watched them.

In the blazing light they recoiled in fright. They flapped aimlessly around, totally dazed and disorientated by the blinding beam. He felt a twinge of guilt but it did no harm; after all, they were only butterflies.

Lorna, Robert's partner of many years, had no interest in his butterflies and indeed not much interest in him either. He spent most evenings in the shed where he was sometimes visited by his friends in the village with similar interests. They had formed a local branch of the Lepidopterology Society. His wife said these lepidopterists were a bunch of weirdos with nothing better to do and on bad days she was known to refer to them as 'lepers' for short. This evening he was expecting Mandy, the treasurer, to pop across with the accounts, but it was raining so hard that he wondered if she would actually turn up. However, Mandy braved the elements and duly tapped on the front door of his house, clutching a page of accounts in a polythene bag. Lorna directed her to the shed with a dismissive gesture.

'You know where he is, Mandy. He's already been there for half an hour gawking at those ruddy butterflies.'

Mandy, by now soaked to the skin with rain dripping off her little nose, trudged up the car track at the side of the house and entered the low-lit shed. Robert felt a wave of appreciation pass over him that she had bothered coming out on an evening like this and she sensed his gratitude as he carefully took her wet anorak and hung it up. Her blouse was soaking wet too so she undid the buttons and slipped out of it, handing it too him. She saw his utter surprise but it merely drove her on to loosen her blue bra, which was hardly wet at all. He timidly placed his arm about her for a moment while he assessed this new development which was way beyond his experience briefing. There was nothing about this in the Society guidance and rules. Then he overcame the butterflies in his stomach, and they sunk towards the old settee in the corner, randomly discarding clothes all over the shed.

In the chaos the cage he was examining was knocked over. The butterflies fluttered out through the cage door and kept landing on them everywhere, but they hardly noticed.

But then the shed's dim light suddenly went out. He struggled up in the darkness and peered out of the window. Everywhere was black and he realised it must be a power cut.

'Lorna will be here in a moment to see if we are okay,' he whispered. 'We'd better get dressed.'

But he need not have worried. Mandy was already panicking and stumbling around the shed in the sheer blackness feeling around for her skirt and bra. His shirt was inside out, and the belt of his trousers became entangled with the wires of the upturned butterfly cage. They bumped into each other several times and the butterflies kept landing on them and getting caught in their clothing.

'Are you two alright in there? It's so wet and dark everywhere,' shouted Lorna from the end of the drive at the house.

They froze for a second, then he shouted back in as normal a voice as he could muster:

'Thanks, we'll be out in a jiffy, just closing the butterfly cages.'

Mandy was half-dressed and whispered:

'I've got the essentials on and I'll just run for it while it's still so dark. You can tell her I've just gone straight back home to see if everything is okay.'

'Good,' he said. 'I'm almost there and I'll sort out my shirt and things as I go back to the house, so we'll just leave together.'

They opened the door, him with his shirt hanging loose and her in a wet blouse clutching a crumpled bra, and stepped out into the pouring rain.

At that moment Lorna, thinking she was doing the right thing, switched on the car headlamps to shine with full intensity up the track and onto the shed door.

In the blazing light they recoiled in fright. They flapped aimlessly around totally dazed and disorientated by the blinding beam. He felt more than a twinge of guilt but then, after all, they were only folk.

Rover Man

THIS MAY BE totally unfair to the majority of Rover drivers, but the term 'Rover Man' has become synonymous with a certain type of potential buyer at our classic car dealership. It originated with a visit from – we'll call him Reginald, whom I collected from our local railway station one damp and dreary November morning. He had informed us he would be carrying a small leather case and there was indeed only one passenger alighting with such a case.

'Good morning, you must be Reginald. I hope you had a good journey from Manchester yesterday and your accommodation in Edinburgh was satisfactory.'

'Yes, it was fine, thank you and I enjoyed a very full breakfast including bacon, eggs, tomato, mushrooms, fried haggis and black pudding topped by lashings of brown sauce. I even followed it with Dundee marmalade, thick cut you know, and two slices of brown bread.'

Certainly a very full breakfast description, I thought, but steered the conversation to the matter in hand.

'I've brought the Rover to the station so that you can experience the short drive back to our premises. It's running well in spite of its 60 years.'

He peered across at the car park and quickly focused on the gleaming Rover P5b Coupe in dove-grey with a white roof and Rostyle wheels. He had studied our photos on the website. As he approached the car he commented:

'I'm surprised you were happy to venture out in it when the roads are so damp and muddy.'

I chose to ignore this remark and concentrated on adjusting the choke so that it started well. We glided out of the carpark and the beautiful 3.5 litre engine produced a characteristic V8 rumble as it picked up speed along the short journey to our office and warehouse. I thought he was impressed (indeed *I* was) that this old lady of over 60 could perform so effortlessly even when fairly cold, but he seemed more intent on peering at the array of dials.

'Do they all work as if they were new?' he enquired.

'Yes, they seem to. The fuel gauge sticks a little and might need a tap because the car has been used so little that the float in the tank is probably a little erratic.'

Once driven into the warehouse he produced an old-fashioned pen-torch with a magnifying glass and commenced an exhaustive assessment.

'I'll be at least couple of hours or so inspecting the car, so perhaps you could lay out all the documents in the office as I need to have 100 per cent proof that the car odometer is correct.'

A horrible thought struck me:

'You appreciate the reading of 5284 miles means it has covered roughly 105 thousand miles as it will have been round the clock in its 60 years?'

'Oh yes, but I want a complete record of its history; you did say in the advert it had much history with it.'

As I retreated to the office, I again offered him coffee.

'Later, later perhaps,' he muttered absentmindedly as he lifted out the back seat and shone the torch on the layer of ancient dust.

I laid out an assortment of the key documents and receipts on a table in the office and proceeded to do some other things, including making myself a coffee. After a couple of hours, I returned to find him lying underneath the car attaching a small magnet to some part of the chassis metalwork, so I crept away, leaving him to it. By the afternoon he did accept a coffee and biscuit, so I tentatively broached the subject of the likelihood of him becoming its new owner. The time he had spent on the inspection and its below-market price encouraged me to think he must be interested.

'I've discovered some failings in the car which detract from its desirability for me. The driver's seat leather is somewhat worn, the chrome on the lower part of one of the over-riders on the back bumper is a little stained and engine is a quite dirty underneath.'

'Well, it is quite old,' I interjected, but he just ignored me and continued with a long list of minor automobile peccadillos, so I slowly finished my coffee and let him prattle on. I have learnt over the years how to use time usefully by thinking about other things in such situations. Twenty minutes later I came to and again risked an interruption.

'I don't think you will find a better Rover P5 on the market.' I ventured.

He looked up from his notes:

'But I shall continue to look for one nevertheless.'

I realised then it was a lost cause. Out of frustrated curiosity I asked him how many others he had inspected.

'Well, you see, over the years I've travelled all over the country from the North of Scotland to Cornwall searching for one that meets my requirements. My wife used to say I was being over-meticulous but now she encourages me to ensure every aspect of the car is correct and totally original. Detail is so important, don't you agree? I typically spend a day or two away and she is very supportive and books the trains and hotels and even encourages me to stay away for longer. She says that she can manage quite well when I'm away on these ventures; it's so kind of her.

'If you wouldn't mind running me back to the station it would be appreciated. There's a train back into Edinburgh at 3.49pm.'

'Are you getting a train from Edinburgh to Manchester tonight, then?'

'Oh no, I'm staying at the George Hotel for another night; the meals there are excellent and I've discovered a really nice Rioja on their house list. I do enjoy a drink when I go away.'

I really need a drink too, I thought.

I ran him back in the imperfect Rover P5 to the local station. As he left, he said:

'By the way, I forgot to mention, if you fold down the passenger sun visor, you'll see that the silvering on the back of the vanity mirror is tarnished. So easy to miss these little things.'

I watched the train leave until it was out of view and lingered a little on the platform. As I drove out of the station, I noticed a train ticket to Manchester lying on the passenger seat. So easy to miss these little things.

Messaging on Mars

IT HAD BEEN a long day of celebrations in the new Colony and Rev. Steve McKay was sitting alone in the corner of the Mars Bar feeling somewhat contemplative. After a year the Colony was becoming increasingly independent of the home planet. The band's finale was a bawdy song with the Chorus:

> *Earth says we run and we run*
> *Earth says we're not here for fun*
> *They mucked up their Planet*
> *And now those who run it*
> *Endeavour to muck up this one.*

Steve had participated in the celebrations with enthusiasm but was feeling uncomfortable at this turn of events, especially when they mispronounced 'mucked' and 'muck'. After all, he was the chaplain. Some rejection of home authority was to be expected in any colony but it was exacerbated by the difficulty of messaging between Mars and Earth owing to a fundamental problem which Steve had to get straight in his mind.

It was at this point that Sid entered the bar and noticed Steve in the corner. He purchased two half pints of what passed for beer and joined him.

'Here you are. You look as if you need replenishing; what's on your mind?'

'It's you scientists and your limitation on the speed of

light. It means we can't speak to folk on Earth, that's the problem.'

'Wow, hold on; we only report on these things. It's your God that fixed it.'

'Are you admit He exists, then', said Steve on cue. 'But explain to me exactly why it's fixed.'

'Look, however advanced the technology, interplanetary communication is encumbered with the difficulty that its speed is limited to the speed of light. That's the highest speed any electronic wave can be propagated and a fundamental tenet of our universe. In 1983 a committee of international scientists recognised the value of this speed as about 186,000 miles per second.'

'A hundred years ago they said the atom could not be split,' interrupted Steve.

'That's completely different because the atom is not fundamentally the smallest division. The fact is: *the speed of light is a fundamental characteristic of the universe. As such it can never be altered.*'

Steve sniffed, but Sid continued.

'I admit any such statement is often seen as arrogant by those not schooled in the concepts of science. What right have scientists to pontificate on these things and come up with such a restriction? This is particularly so with many of your religious colleagues because they argue that God is omnipotent and can do anything, including alter the speed of light if He so wishes. Such an argument, though, is ingenuous and actually disrespectful to your God.'

He took another sip of beer and, as Steve said nothing, carried on.

'For example, the sum of 1 plus 2 is indisputably 3. To say that an all-powerful God can make it equal to 4 reduces God to some trickster. The same could be said of the circumference of a circle being approximately 3.14 times its diameter, the sum of the squares of adjacent sides of a right-angled triangle being the square of the hypotenuse and so on and the speed of light being 186,000 miles per second. It is perfectly rational to say God does exist or that He does not; whatever the truth, both statements could form the basis of a reasonable argument. What is not meaningful is to say that God made an irrational universe. That would be saying God can alter facts such as 1 plus 2 equals 3, the circumference of a circle divided by the diameter is 3.14 or the speed of light.'

Steve knew this was right and knew it was uncomfortable for some of his more enthusiastic theological colleagues because it seemingly limited their God, but he said nothing, as Sid was drifting into a lecturing mode.

'This limitation on the speed of light (and all waves in space) has practical implications for Mars. Being an average of 140 million miles away, a simple sum shows that on average it takes about 12 minutes for electronic waves to travel to or from Mars. That means if you're on Mars and you're rolling pastry for an apple pie and you ring your mum about the required oven time, the message takes 12 minutes to get to her, 5 minutes or so for her to reply and 12 minutes for her answer to come back; roughly half an hour in total. The conclusion must be that it's difficult to rely on Earth for any practical short-term help (and that you should download a cook book before you go).

'This explains why "Communication" adds a further reason why the government of the Mars community must be local and self-sufficient. No doubt the authorities on Earth will be less than happy about this, as indeed were the government departments in London with the gradual independence of their American Colonies a hundred years ago. Put another way, the half-hour communication lag not only means it is impossible to have a normal conversation or Zoom chat but more importantly that any timely response to an unexpected event on Mars cannot be made from the Earth. Thus, for logistic and safety reasons, control on Mars has to be self-contained and local.'

Steve had drifted; he was thinking about his mum and apple pie.

'So that's why when messaging my mum I have to make a wee holographic presentation which is then transmitted to her and watched by her 12 minutes or so later and for her to then do the same in response. It makes for very stilted communication and not conversation as we know it. It's rather like sending telegrams in the old days.'

'That's right and it means that in all those space fiction books you read and in the *Star Wars* films you watch, when there's conversation with folk on Earth ("Beam me up, Scotty") it's actually not possible. Not that it matters too much because that's all fiction and it would be a pity to spoil a good story. Furthermore, it's impossible, not because we haven't got the technology yet but because it would contravene a *fundamental law of the universe*.'

'Like buying rounds in turn,' Sid added, 'peering into his empty plastic beaker.'

Seeing Is Believing

WAYNE WORSHIPPED WIKIPEDIA. He had been using it for five years; that was half his lifetime. It gave him authoritative answers to all those questions that seemed to weary the adults that he asked.

'Where do blackbirds go in the winter, Mum?'
'When did the dodo become extinct?'
'Is the blue whale endangered?' And so on.

He loved animals almost as much as he loved his iPad but while iPads were everywhere, there were very few animals around him in the sprawling suburbs of Los Angeles. There was always the local zoo which was not too bad as zoos go but he had been so many times he reckoned the animals now recognised him. Indeed, last time he visited, he was sure the chimpanzees nudged one and other and made derogatory remarks about him, sending them into squawking giggles.

The information boards were all so patronising too:

Here is the Indian Elephant. Country of Origin: India. Habitat: open savanna shrub land. Did you know the Indian Elephant has smaller ears than the African Elephant... Of course I did, it would look stupid if it didn't as it's often half its size. Its trunk is shorter too... blah, blah, blah.

So, the zoo was now ditched in favour of wildlife documentaries, but even these were becoming wearisome, especially the ones that gave all the animals human characteristics and emotions. 'Anthropomorphising' was the fancy word some wildlife book had used but he just called it stupid, as animals' brains are just wired differently. Was there no way of getting to know animals without access being screened by human interference?

Then one summer, out of the blue his mother announced that they were going on an African safari to the Maasai Mara reserve to see the animals. He could hardly believe it and would have given her a hug had she not been driving the big Chevrolet in thick Los Angeles traffic at the time. Furthermore, she explained, they would have to stay in a wooden ranch and the brochure said there may be insects and monkeys around them at night. It sounded idyllic to Wayne and indeed would have been except for one thing, his Mum's voice.

I first met Wayne and his mother at breakfast on the first day of the tour. She was giving a very loud Californian commentary on each item offered in the breakfast bar.

'Wayne, you should try these thorny Durian fruit, we can't get them in LA you know.'

'Somebody has taken the milk, you'll have to make do without cereal as there's none left.'

And then, turning to me, 'I'm showing Wayne the animals you know, he's always wanted to see them…' And so on and so forth.

It continued during our first trip out from the ranch.

'This Land Rover's very basic and noisy. It's even more bumpy than your yellow school bus, it will frighten the animals away.' Mention of his yellow school bus was the last thing Wayne wanted to be broadcast.

He had tried sitting by himself but she always plonked herself down next to him and rambled on. His mum she might be, kind she might be; but her never-ending commentary to all within earshot was mighty irritating.

One evening at dinner a few days later, about a dozen or so of us were seated around the table on the raised veranda overlooking the surrounding shrub land. By then we had seen some of the 'big ones': the lion, the elephant, the leopard and the giraffe, but not the rhinoceros. We were relaxed and had become acquainted with one and other sufficiently well to be comfortable. I noticed that Wayne's mum was much quieter now and surmised he must have expressed his frustration to her at some point.

Suddenly though, she stood up, nearly knocking over the table and pointed excitedly.

'Well, just look at that, there's a white gorilla out there in the distance by that dark bush on the left. Look, you can see it move.'

Wayne rolled his eyes, sighed and then searched for white gorilla on his iPhone. His mum hurried to the edge of the veranda and was peering excitedly at the undergrowth some 100 metres away.

'It's the sun's reflection,' somebody said.

'No, it's not, there it is again quite clearly stomping about. I tell you it's a white gorilla.'

By now Wayne had found *white gorilla* in Wikipedia and discovered there was only one albino gorilla and it had been in Barcelona Zoo. He squinted at it; his young eyes must have seen more than most and it certainly appeared to be a gorilla and more or less white. He was totally confused and regaled his mum with:

'It cannot possibly be a white gorilla because that would mean Wikipedia is wrong. It must be a hoax or the evening light or something.'

The next morning Wayne was down early at breakfast by himself so I joined him.

'Mum has overslept,' he said by way of explanation.

As we munched our cereals together, there being plenty

of milk that early, I showed him the electronic picture I had taken the previous evening using my Nikon single-lens-reflex camera with its high-powered telephoto lens. The white gorilla was clearly visible. He did not say anything so I went on to explain:

'I had a chat with the camp manager. He told me he had only seen an albino gorilla once before but had been told by the rangers there were three of them out there.'

I sent the picture to his email and he agreed to inform Wikipedia of this new discovery and forward the picture as evidence.

'That's how information works,' I told him.

'Information sources ranging from Wikipedia to your mum all need constantly updating in the light of experience, you know.'

He was pensive for a moment, then added with a grin, 'And a posh camera with a long lens helps too.'

London Smog

DURING THE WEEK there was a BBC Four documentary about the great winter freeze of 1962-63. Temperatures dropped below minus 20 degrees, the whole country became snowbound and everything came to a standstill. It lasted from December until the beginning of March, creating conditions we would now call lockdown. Global warming would have been a distant dream. In 1720 it was even colder; however bad a situation may be, it has always been worse at some point in the past.

I was a young student in London at the time, living in a red brick Victorian flat with several other wet-behind-the-ears teenage students from sheltered backgrounds. It was located in Stoke Newington, which was conveniently placed a few miles north of City University (since absorbed by London University). The rent was reasonable for London owing to Stoke Newington at the time being less than salubrious. We were surrounded by seedy sawdust pubs, local shops that still sold biscuits in brown paper bags and chippies that supplied a greasy poke wrapped in the *Daily Mirror*. The flat upstairs was occupied by two ladies who offered, according to their advert on the door, *trouser-pressing while you wait*, which was odd because we never notice any guys with neat creases.

It was very cold although, strangely enough, it was not the freezing temperature which remains in my memory but rather the stifling fog, or smog as they called it, during the week before the cold spell. Those who never experienced a London pea-souper smog may find it difficult to believe the sheer claustrophobic terror of the choking, puce-coloured cloud which completely displaces the surrounding air. Even walking along a pavement is difficult because vision is limited to the edge of a globe around your head like an extended space helmet. You cannot see your feet, so you instinctively shuffle to avoid curbs. Passers-by can be heard, their coughs oddly amplified by the smog, but only seen vaguely as their globe fleetingly brushes through yours. Lamplights offer a smoky hue which only makes visibility worse. Many old people and those with underlying medical conditions died from smog inhalation in the December of 1962, less than the one in 1953 when there were 12,000 fatalities, but nevertheless one of the worst. Over the period the smog was as devastating as the recent pandemic. As it happens, both were brought under control by man's intervention, these being the Clean Air Act and vaccination.

It was under such conditions that I set out late that afternoon from an engineering drawing class at the university to walk the few miles home to Stoke Newington. My duffle coat soon became sodden and I felt cold and miserable. Each time I came to a tube station entrance I considered using the Northern Line to make my journey back to the flat, but reports of dangerously crowded platforms (as there were no buses running) and choking tube trains dissuaded me. I had been walking about an hour when I tripped over what appeared to be a grey coat lying near a wall and just managed to right myself. I looked back and realised to my horror that it was a person lying there. I resisted the primeval instinct to hurry away and went back to investigate. The coat concealed an elderly lady, fortunately alive as I saw her eyes move, but obviously stunned and disorientated. I surmised she must have tripped over a curb or paving stone.

I bent down and asked if I could help. She appeared not to register my presence, so I bent closer and just heard her say:

'Are you speaking to me?'

'Yes, are you hurt?

She stared for a moment and whispered, 'I'm really not sure, I just stumbled and fell.' She moved her hands and feet a little. 'Everything seems to work but I've bruised my head, I'm sure. Here, help me up and I'll see how I am, laddie. I only live a few doors away down the street.'

A man wearing a brown trilby hat was passing and noticed what I was doing. The two of us helped her to her feet but she was decidedly unsteady.

'Best to sit her down and let her collect her thoughts before she goes off,' he whispered to me.

There was nowhere to sit her down and we wondered what to do. Parked nearby there was an old black saloon car, possibly a Daimler or similar and I tried the back door – it was not locked. The doors of such cars were locked by clicking up each internal handle in turn – quite a hassle for the driver to stretch back and check before locking the driver's door and thus often left unclasped.

'You cannot sit her in there,' said trilby man, 'that's somebody's car.'

'Why not? It's an emergency and she's unlikely to be there long,' I argued.

After a little struggle, we managed to seat her on the back seat which I noticed was shiny brown leather with an ample armrest in the centre.

She just sat for a moment or two and then to our relief began to perk up a little and absorb her plush and comfortable surroundings.

'What do I do if the owner or his driver comes by?' she enquired anxiously.

I hesitated; she was obviously well to do; very few owners had 'drivers' in 1962. But then I was only a naïve young student, and all this was well beyond my experience span. I was about to attempt a suitably caring and reassuring answer when trilby man said:

'Well, dear' – *slightly patronising but allowable in 1962* – 'if you're recovered by then you can either make a run for it or give him your price.'

I was dumbstruck that he would say such a thing, but she stared at him for a second and burst out laughing – and then we all laughed together.

After a while she very carefully extracted herself from the car but seemed stable enough once standing up again. She thanked us both and we all continued on our separate ways in the dense grey smog, in my case feeling a little less gloomy than before.

Coal Man

COAL IS USUALLY found at the bottom of a mine rather than at the bottom of a teacup. I had found this care home of mine quite attentive to cleanliness and that dark nurse with long hair they call Sarah showed no unusual concern as she laid the China cup and saucer beside my chair. I gave up sugar long ago but do have a splash of milk which Sarah had already added. Sipping tea is a soothing experience; most of my life it had been from an enamel mug rather than a China cup but nevertheless most enjoyable. However, on this occasion as the level dropped it was totally shattered by the discovery of a lump of jet-black coal about an inch cube in size lurking in the bottom.

Now I know I go on a bit about working down the old pit at Monktonhall and the hard lives of all those poor miners, but who would do such a thing in this posh home full of respectable folk? I drew it to the attention of Sarah who was highly amused; okay, I suppose it's a little funny, but she denied any knowledge of the perpetrator. I lay awake that night and wondered if I'd gone on about coal too much and who it could be that took the trouble to obtain the coal, hopefully wash it and surreptitiously drop it in my tea. I kept on at Sarah who continued to deny withholding any information but did finally mention in passing that there was a retired and somewhat reclusive coal man in the superior rooms upstairs. This was the first I had heard of another coal man in this very home and I asked her to invite him to meet me for a chat in the common area. 'Coal Man' is the term normally used for those who deliver it in bags, but I deemed he must have graduated to being a successful coal merchant or something, having one of the grand rooms upstairs.

I heard nothing for a couple of days until one morning Sarah informed me that the Coal Man would be having coffee in the common area at 11 am and would make himself available. Well, I thought, I'd better be 'available' too as I had made the suggestion. I had been thinking of a wee chat rather than anything more formal but duly presented myself at the correct time, slightly tidied up and my hair, such as it was, brushed. He was sitting in the corner clad in an old tweed jacket which almost camouflaged with the ancient chair. He looked somewhat vacant but also strangely familiar to me. I was beckoned to a seat beside him in an authoritative manner and accepted the coffee he offered, from a cafetiere indeed. Those in the upper rooms receive very special perks, it seems.

I explained that I had been a miner for many years in a local pit and was surprised they had not mentioned there was another miner in the home. I admitted the mine was my favourite topic of conversation and relayed the recent incident of the coal in my tea cup. He expressed no opinion about the incident but started to question me about my time as a miner. On this I could wax eloquent, and I gave him the unexpurgated account of how, only 50 years ago, over half a million miners covered in black dust spent their best years slaving (for it was a form of slavery) for the National Coal Board. East Lothian alone had many thousands including around 2000 at Monktonhall when I was there. I told him I would never forget the ends of their shifts when they came up from the seams covered in black dust and their eyes dilated, giving them an eerie stare as they emerged into the bright light.

'I know,' he said, 'I was involved in ending it once and for all.'

I looked at him again and with a shock it dawned on me who he was. I could think of nothing to say. This weathered, kindly old man before me was none other than Jimmy what's his name, one time head of the Scottish Coal Board I believe and colleague of Sir Ian MacGregor at the National Coal Board, who famously faced off Arthur Scargill in the miners' strikes and refused to give them the rise they were demanding.

'Sorry, I should perhaps have introduced myself,' he said, 'but you hardly gave me a chance.'

I'm afraid, as a former member of Mike McGahey's boys, I did not rise to the occasion and ended up asking him how he came to be in this home. He explained how he had been involved in mine pit design early in his life (I'd heard he was a brilliant mining engineer) and moved into management and up the ladder. I asked him if he received honours and such things, but it turned out he just faded away, as deputies do after taking all the flak. I remembered a favourite tale at the National Union of Mineworkers at the time was that he would never be granted a knighthood because, when the Queen touched his shoulder with the sword and said, 'Arise, Sir James,' he would revert to form and say, 'A rise? No, I will never allow a rise.'

His eyes were boring into me and I felt he knew what I was thinking. Here was the man in charge with others of closing the pits. Seventy were closed by the NCB at that time, more or less as predicted by Scargill but fervently denied by Thatcher and that Tory government. The mine with its dark steel towers and winding wheels was the very life-blood of their existence; they had never known any other life in the mining villages. More British miners lost their livelihood, their *raison d'etre*, their very spirits, at that time than all those British people who perished in the Second World War. They are the forgotten army of humanity emerging coal-black and tired from holes in the ground to provide energy for the lifestyles of those above – but sorry, I'm drifting away here.

We spoke amicably enough about those times and agreed we both had a job to do and did it as best we could. He was getting tired and seemed to be in some discomfort.

'Come back in a day or two,' he said. 'At least it will relieve the monotony of this bloody home.'

I'd forgotten to ask him about the coal in my tea and decided next time to press him on the matter; it must surely have been him. A member of the National Coal Board, one of those who could implement a programme of pit closures and deny it to half a million miners, would surely have no scruples about arranging for a lump of coal to be placed in one of their tea cups.

If so, was it a message, a grudging acceptance that coal and those that slaved to extract it, would forever be submerged under a veneer of respectable text-book history? What could symbolise it better than a lump of coal below the surface of a British cup of tea?

Unfortunately, I shall never know the answer because he passed away peacefully in the night.

News Release

THE CREW HAD known since the beginning of the trip to Mars about the potential landing problem and had indeed been working on solutions. Essentially, one of the four extending landing legs of the Drove spacecraft had been damaged on lift-off. They were sworn to secrecy by the Mars Council. The weak link in the information security was, as always in such situations, the avoidance of any hint by the crew to their loved ones on Earth. The odd innuendo – 'If we get back okay', 'If you could transfer our savings to another account', 'If anything happens, I love you' – could signal a slight concern. The sum total of all this apprehension over a period could seed a suspicion and lead to anxious questions about the mission from those that knew them best. And it was indeed thus, that one evening a tired crew member hinted to his girlfriend on Earth that there was a mechanical problem needing to be resolved before landing.

She is a sharp girl and couples it with the flame flare which was reported at the launch. Indeed, it could be seen in some of the released pictures. So she twitters her buddies in the Mission Friends Group consisting of friends and associates of the crew. The tweet only says, 'Looks like damage to Drove could cause a landing problem,' but it's enough to seed panic within the Friends Group.

When accidentally leaked to terrestrial social media it was seized upon with alacrity by the press, who were suffering from a quiet news day and needed a good headline:

Drove in Peril as it nears Mars.

Rev Steve McKay, the mission chaplain, noticed it and quickly perused the article. It actually had very little of substance and neither disclosed the reason for the peril nor its potential effect on landing the craft. Steve decided to see the captain immediately but was met by one of the captain's assistants, who seemed to have adopted the task of shielding him. Steve convinced him of the urgency without disclosing too much and was ushered into the captain's office a few minutes later.

Captain Peter Reid knew about the news release and was exasperated that somebody had leaked it in spite of his request. Like many precise and well-ordered people, he had difficulty managing unexpected events. Steve pointed out that it was probably no one person alone and certainly not intentional. The captain thought it was important that all eighty or so passengers in the spacecraft were informed immediately before they saw it on line and that they were given assurance about the ongoing work on a resolution to the problem. He then, to Steve's surprise, asked Steve to make the announcement.

Steve immediately suggested it should come from the captain himself, but Captain Reid explained that was not the way he wanted it done as it would cause too much concern at this stage. He insisted that Steve as chaplain should inform them immediately that there had been an unfortunate news release on earth which exaggerated the problems with the landing gear and that the chaplain would make himself available to assist any of the passengers or crew who were apprehensive, either on their own behalf or because of the effect on their families. The captain did, however, offer Steve one of the crew members, Sid Hawthorn, as a press officer to assist him on technical questions.

Steve left to consider how he would inform his colleagues without signalling a doomsday scenario. After dinner that evening, he proceeded to a corner at the top of the stairs between the two levels in the spacecraft (dubbed speaker's corner by the cynics), picked up the microphone and gave the following announcement:

Colleagues,

May I please have your attention for a few moments. The captain has asked me to speak to you about the Terrestrial news item doing the rounds this morning in many of the national electronic newspapers. Some of you may already have picked it up. It relates to the accidental flare released by one of the engines on our launch which has left one of the landing legs slightly damaged. The crew, under guidance from Mission Control on Earth and the Mars Council here, are trying to repair the faulty leg, mainly at night when other systems are using little power; you may have heard mechanical noises in the distance.

As always, the press has sensationalised this by considering the worst-case scenario and this may lead to folk at home, including your own families and friends, becoming concerned. I would like to assure you that solutions are being devised, and once perfected there is no need to assume landing will not be as smooth as it has been on the previous occasions. You may remember that previous landings were very uneventful and their crews were commended.

Finally, I am happy to assist any of you who have concerns individually or within your families, including, as chaplain, *praying with you for a safe journey and arrival on Mars. I am happy to take questions but bear in mind I'm not a technical guy and will, therefore, deflect any questions on such detail to Sid here, the crew member in charge of landing arrangements.*

There was silence for a moment, a lull before the storm, and then the questions started. Most of them had been suffering from acute boredom and while concerned, it at least added a new dimension of interest and excitement. They came thick and fast: why had they not been kept abreast of progress, why had two months gone by before Earthlings were told, why was the design dependent on legs anyway, what happened if it fell over? And so on. And then, why are *you*, rather than the captain, telling us and what's this about praying? – Even if it worked on Earth it's hardly going to work in space. 'We want more information,' they said, 'so get us some answers and next time, bring the captain with you.'

Over the next few days, several of them sought Steve's advice on dealing with their concerned families and one or two on private matters which at least gave Steve the satisfaction of feeling that his odd role as chaplain was beginning to be accepted. However, this did not diminish his own inner concern about how they were going to land this stricken vessel on the rocky Mars terrain.

Rocket Power

JOSEPH WAS STANDING on the edge of the crowd with his cloth cap and his young son Benjamin.

'I'll lift you up when the Rocket appears,' he promised.

Even as he spoke a reverberating rumble could be heard from far away and the crowd became silent. Ben was jittery with excitement, but all he could see as he looked up was a patch of sky between all the heads and shoulders towering above him. He knew, though, that his father would place him on his shoulders when the action started. After all, it was a mind-blowing occasion: he would see with his own eyes the large metal Rocket that his father had told him about. It had so much power it would carry nearly 100 people on its first mission.

He did not have to wait long. Joseph detected a wisp of silver-grey vapour in the far distance.

'Time you had a grandstand view,' he said as he lifted Benjamin right up and made him comfortable with his legs straddling his neck and his hands clutching his cap. More bursts of vapour appeared behind the foreground trees and dissipated into the surrounding sky. The rumbling became louder. Ten, nine, eight, and the noise became more pronounced. Seven, six, five: the whole crowd rose a little as everybody stood on tiptoe and strained to see. Four, three, two, and there seemed to be a moment of utter concentration as it emerged into view. Behind the black metal cylinder, a glimpse of red-hot fire could be seen between the clouds of vapour billowing into the afternoon sky. A gasp of wonder emanated from the crowd at the mechanical might and sheer force of this, the greatest of man's inventions. It seemed to wee Ben that its power was dominating the entire countryside. Did it have a right to do this? Would things ever be the same again now that a hundred folk could be propelled away in such a contraption?

As it pursued its prescribed course, hidden on occasions by the billowing smoke and steam, the crowd watched with awe until it gradually moved out of view. There followed a reflective pause and then much apprehensive murmuring among the crowd. Ben was carefully lifted down to ground level where he once again found himself surrounded by baggy trousers and long dresses with petticoats peeping out and he reached up to hold his father's hand.

On the way home, his father's keen sense of occasion seemed to be fired up like the Rocket they had witnessed. It led to Ben being given an informative lecture about its significance.

'Ben, you must remember this event and the date of 15th September 1830. You are lucky enough to have seen Robert Stephenson's locomotive, The Rocket, on its first scheduled journey carrying fare-paying passengers along an iron road all the way from Liverpool to Manchester. This steam engine has the power because it has lots of tubes to carry the hot gases from the fire through the boiler rather than just heating it below. This means it produces lots and lots of steam for the two pistons at the sides. Such inventions by great engineers will eventually transform the way mankind travels and the way the goods we make can be traded across the country.'

But Ben was getting tired and he had a stone in his shoe. It was not until 50 years later, when every self-respecting town in Britain and many villages had a railway station, that the significance really sunk in.

Maybe, 200 years later, Ben's descendants will view another rocket, one that wings its way to Mars with a hundred folk on board; a short time-lapse in the great scheme of things.

Last Piece

THE RESPECTED EDINBURGH solicitors of William McKay and Partners WS had occupied premises just off George Street in Edinburgh for over 100 years. On the second floor just at the top of the marble stairway there was an impressive room originally used by the founder, William McKay, himself. While the staff of the time always referred to their senior partner, in his presence, as Mr McKay, it became popularly known among them as Will's room. These days it is still called Will's room and possibly by association it has become the room used for reading the wills of the deceased. The documents would be spread out over the large oval mahogany table in the centre which by its very presence elicited a sense of occasion. Today, though, the table would be used for a purpose it had never experienced before.

Six months or so previously, a Mr Sidney Archer, an East Lothian farmer, had visited the solicitors to arrange an amendment to his will following the discovery that he was terminally ill. The will bestowed his estate, mainly his farm and some valuable investments from way back, to his three sons and one daughter, his wife having predeceased him by several years. His children had all left the family farm years before and were living their own lives in different parts of the country. He often met and stayed with them individually but he was disappointed that they had grown apart from each another and now hardly ever met their fellow siblings. Like many parents, he liked to think of them keeping in contact with each other and thus keeping the family unit alive. It would at least mean the memory of their happy times together in the past was perpetuated for the next generation. It was not that there was any animosity between them beyond the odd tiff now and then and he had accepted that none of them wanted to run the farm, but rather the absence of family connectedness that concerned him.

He had died in a hospice and his grieving family had been requested to assemble early in the morning in the Wills Room where Mr Arbuckle, a junior partner of the firm, was officiating. Following some preliminary polite condolences and legal reminders, Mr Arbuckle, complete with gold-rimmed spectacles and an important-looking buff folder, explained that the deceased had made a late alteration to his will:

'You may be surprised to learn that key investment documents have been hidden by your father and that the clue to their whereabouts is contained in a jigsaw puzzle which I have to hand.'

The siblings were incredulous and asked one another and then Mr Arbuckle why ever their father would do that.

'I've no idea,' said Mr Arbuckle as he peered over his spectacles. 'However, you have no option but to assemble the puzzle, which I'm afraid has 1000 parts.'

With that he poured all the cardboard pieces onto the oval table and left them to it. Never has a large puzzle been assembled so quickly but it still took until mid-afternoon. They fought and bickered as they would have done when children many years before. Finally, after numerous coffees provided gratis by the solicitors, they were down to the last few pieces.

The picture portrayed one of the farmhouse rooms with their father sitting in his special chair; he must have sent a photograph away to have it made into a jigsaw. They were now down to the last piece – except it wasn't quite, as there seemed to be a piece missing. There was a frantic hunt but to no avail and there was certainly no obvious clue to any documents. It was Geoffrey, the eldest, who suggested that maybe this was the point: the documents were located where the piece was missing. The vacant jigsaw space was part of a bookcase where some old books that nobody ever moved were kept. Anthony piped up:

'We'll have to go back to the house and look in that area.'

They hurriedly arranged their transport to East Lothian after giving the nonplussed Mr Arbuckle a short explanation and promising to return the next day. Elsie had no transport as she had come up from London, so Geoffrey gave her a lift and she felt a fraternal cosiness at the prospect of sitting next to her older brother again in a big Land Rover. Ian, the youngest brother, having an old Maserati, offered to take Anthony so that 'he could have a ride in a decent car'! They arrived first and had to endure the young-tearaway jibes from the others. It was akin to 'The Famous Five' exploits, except there were four and they were in their 50s, and even 60s in Geoffrey's case.

Sure enough, one of the large books in the location of the missing piece was hollowed out and contained lots of share certificates and stock records. At the bottom lurked a solitary piece of the jigsaw. They went down to the local inn to celebrate and after a glorious evening ended up abandoning their cars and spending some of their newfound fortune on a taxi ride back to their various hotels in Edinburgh. The next morning, they met again round the oval table and mock-ceremoniously placed the missing piece in position in the presence of Mr Arbuckle. The will was formally disposed, and they had a parting coffee in the nearby Café Royale.

It was Elsie who suggested that they should meet up in Edinburgh occasionally without their other halves and any children to repeat the evening. They readily agreed and she added:

'Why ever would Dad do such a crazy thing? – We might have cleared the house and never found the shares and the puzzle piece.'

'He must have been losing it at the end, just mildly perhaps,' said Geoffrey.

'Yes, I suppose we'll never know,' said Anthony as he clambered into a taxi and waved them goodbye.

Falling out of Grace

MANY YEARS AGO there was there was a stooshie in a wee Highland kirk. The lively young choir mistress had fallen out of grace with some of the church elders, partly because she had successfully enthused and developed the church choir into more than a simple music group and partly because the minister began to view it as a challenge. The choir went from strength to strength – 35, 40, 50 members – and did not suffer from the usual difficulty of attracting men for the tenor and bass parts. The church, on the other hand, had a declining congregation of at best some 50 members to its morning services including the Sunday School children and a solid band of older villagers.

The choir not only sung at the church but elsewhere around the county and were increasingly being sought to perform more broadly to the point where the church became best known for being the home base of the choir. Villagers who would not attend morning services or be involved with a religion did appreciate this aspect of their local church. Faith or no faith, they enjoyed praising the Lord with wonderful fugues and arias which could be heard all over the village on practice nights.

However, general resentment of the choir among some of the less musically-inclined church folk, peppered with disagreements over introits and hymn tunes, erupted at one of the session meetings. Halfway through the meeting, the choir mistress rose to her feet, walked to the front, swept back her dark curls and told the Minister in non-liturgical language exactly why her choir could no longer operate within the stifling constraints placed on them by the church. She then strode purposefully out of the hall, discovering on the way that the door would not slam properly as it had one of those ridiculous metal arms attached to it, went home and sobbed her heart out.

The goodly band of elders were furious that their esteemed minister should be openly challenged in this way and the subsequent whispering campaign led to the choir mistress terminating her eldership, resigning her membership and starting a community choir having no connection with the church. They then turned their attention to her husband who, in supporting her, had voiced a few harsh words about them, and requested that he resign too, although he had served the congregation well over the years. Meanwhile the new community choir proceeded well with the same folk the choir had had before and it nearly settled down again.

However, the offending couple had the effrontery (in the eyes of the elders) to continue attending Sunday services. It was, after all, their family church with many family connections and had been so for several generations. The Minister sought advice from his peer group of neighbouring ministers in the Highlands, one of whom offered to chair an ad hoc meeting of the elders and act as its moderator.

Thus it was that on a Sunday afternoon in August, an ad hoc meeting was constituted with a prayer and the gathering were informed of the purpose, this being to decide what to do about the errant couple. The moderator instructed that no minutes were to be taken and that no word of the meeting was ever to be divulged – it was to be forever a secret. The elders sketched faces to reveal their thoughts, whether sad or happy, about the situation. On swapping the drawings around it was evident that no elders were likely to receive invites from the Scottish Academy; even as emojis they were poor. He opened the floor for discussion by explaining that they should not make derogatory personal remarks about the offending couple. He then proceeded to ask leading questions which induced an abundance of derogatory personal remarks. One elder did ask who was acting in defence of the couple but he was totally ignored, habeas corpus seemingly not applying to session meetings.

Emotional expressions of dissatisfaction with the couple then became the order of the day. Elders brimming with holy indignation questioned their commitment to the church while some women welled up in tears as they meted out the criticisms:

'Did they think they ran the Church.'

'She made me feel small.'

'He sits near the front with his arms folded.'

'She bosses the organist.'

'Heard he was critical of the minister.'

'She totally ignores me.'

And so on and so forth; none major offences in themselves even if they had been true, but as a whole constituting death by a thousand cuts.

Then the possibility was raised of banning them from the church and there followed a general murmur of assent which grew and grew until it became an unholy clamour for such action.

'Ban them, ban them,' they said.

'Ban them for ever from our Church.'

The Elder who had raised the absence of any defence was feeling increasingly uncomfortable and asked:

'What are you all thinking of? There's no mechanism for banning anybody from the Church of Scotland.'

He would have said more but failed on the spur of the moment to find words owing to a momentary relapse into the past. Three hundred years earlier it might have been 'Burn them, burn them,' rather than ban them. Was this the residue of those same black spirits of old still swirling hither and thither in ghostly swathes above the gathering? He felt an involuntary shudder.

The moderator conceded the point, though, and they paused for a moment. But then they regrouped and come back with one elder insisting:

'Then they must be asked to sit at the back, not under the nose of our minister.'

So, this is what they were asked to do – sit in disgrace at the back of their own church. Needless to say, the couple departed for good and it left a great void. In the course of time the incident faded from memory but the declining numbers in the congregation led to that Highland Kirk never again being graced with a full-time minister.

Food for Thought

THE INTERNATIONAL POLITICS unfolding on Earth with respect to the Mars village were in every sense becoming remote to those on Mars. The Earth was approaching its furthest distance from Mars in the cycling of the two planets and this was reflected in the attitude of the villagers. Indeed, they were generally more preoccupied with their immediate surroundings in the Dome, their day-to-day work, housekeeping and, not least, their food than the small globe they sometimes saw in the sky. They did not deny the reality surrounding them, but they preferred to leave the deeper thinking to others. After all, as Plato had observed long ago, you do not want too many thinkers in the marketplace. In fact, it's fair to say that in the overall scheme of things, food for the humans on Mars is equally important as fuel for the rockets; poor food leads to poor functioning and ultimately to poor thinking. You do need – food for thought.

Rev Steve McKay recognised this and took it upon himself as part of his duties to be a champion of better food on Mars. On his earthly pilgrimage (as he loved to call his time before Mars, with a nod to John Bunyan), he had several theories why his home Church of Scotland – and, for that matter, many other establishment-based religions – were losing their flocks. Apart from the deeper matter of belief, there was their poor standard of food and drink. The way to the heart is through the stomach and if God resides in the heart, then food has a religious significance.

The Jews, the Muslims, the Hindus, in fact, many of the really old religions, realised this long ago but it obviously takes thousands of years to appreciate this as some haven't got there yet; food and drink is just not their cup of tea. Whatever your tastes, a *kosher falafel*, an Arabic *moussaka* or a Hindu *vindaloo* are all catalysts to conviviality. Methodist, Baptists and Presbyterians have no dishes which are a patch on these and indeed patronise other cultures whenever they go out for a decent meal. Presbyterians are by far the worst, favouring well-fingered biscuits and instant coffee to wash away their sermons; so unlike their convivial leader 2000 years ago who loved wining and dining with lively discourse and good food. Where did it all go so wrong?

Back on Mars, Steve found there was limited cuisine because there was no incentive to use core ingredients and a lack of ingenuity. Some Italian company had cornered the market in interplanetary packaged food and boasted over 157 varieties wrapped in plastic and brought to soggy life by adding water, which is in any case in short supply on Mars. They can be prepared in five minutes but that's no advantage because the Mars folk have hours of leisure time and nothing to do and nowhere to go. His campaign to get more core food ingredients from Earth was having some effect, but only by assertive action and the threat of strikes. Many of the villagers were aged in their thirties and inspired in their youth by *The Martian* film (from the book by Andy Weir) where a stranded earthling manages to survive by growing vegetables. Indeed, the production of good food can be as satisfying as its consumption.

It was with this in mind that Steve lobbied the council one morning at their weekly executive meeting.

'Before we go,' said the acting president, now widely

abbreviated to AP by the villagers, 'are there any other items which cannot be left until next week?'

'Yes,' piped up Steve, ignoring the AP's *I-want-to-finish* look. 'In view of the increasing problem with boredom and lethargy, requiring pep drugs which are now running low on Mars, I suggest we apportion the growing zone beside Dome B to those who wish to have garden allotments so that they can grow their own food and sell it if desired.'

Steve usually tested out his ideas on his colleagues first, but not this one as he had only just thought of it.

The president, now getting to know Steve well, guessed as much.

'And what is your considered policy on prevention of contamination between the domes, your selection procedure for applicants for these allotments and the pricing structure of the produce?' he asked.

'All in a report which I'll submit in due course.'

Well, it was not quite a lie because he didn't say he'd finalised the report or even started it yet.

'In that case, we'll look forward to receiving it before our meeting next week so that we can consider your report in depth at the meeting,' said the VP as he got up to go.

That evening, as was his wont, Steve tested out his ideas with a generally less-than-convinced audience in the Mars Bar.

Steve dealt with the usual chaplaincy matters over the next few days; advising folk on family issues back on Earth, consoling those who missed family events at home or lost a parent while they were away, arranging weekly Christian and Islamic services as best he could. He was not seen around in the evenings, declined a dinner with his friend Jo and was noticeably absent from the Mars Bar. The reason was that the report on his allotments idea which he thought was probably a non-starter and thus not worthy of much time, had become not only feasible but very attractive. It was finished two days before the next meeting, which gave council members time to study it and him time to have an evening off. Accordingly, he wandered into the Mars Bar to enjoy a well-earned reward and had just ordered when he was surprised to see the AP sitting in the corner by himself. Steve thought he must have rewarded himself too, but his reward must have been for something very special as he hardly ever went there.

Although the AP was known for his somewhat correct and prudish ways, Steve risked a jokingly familiar greeting.

'What brings you here to this den of iniquity so early in the evening?'

'It's hardly that. The surroundings are grim, and I've decided to get rid of that robot and have a full-time rota manning this place, although Earthlings will probably try to prevent it. In answer to your question, it's their petty bickering at every committee meeting that has driven me to seek refuge here. I've spent all day trying to convince their Conveyancing Department to send more core food ingredients. The deadline for finalising consignments is a month before taking off date, why I don't know, and they are still arguing about it. They did agree to send more barley grains among the other things, though.'

'And why barley in particular?' asked Steve.

The AP did not answer but raised his glass of dark stout. Steve realised that Guinness ingredients must be getting low.

'Patrick our brewer is always pestering me to place it on higher priority, but I have to be careful.' He then added, 'We also thought we would try some fruit in the greenhouse. The yield per square metre has to be high to make the case but we are going to experiment with intensive strawberries in layered trays, pineapples and also raspberries as the canes can straddle around other items in unused spaces. Potato plants, on which tomatoes can be grown as well as they are essentially the same plant, have come into their own and we have been asked to test them.'

Steve asked, 'All this along with the existing strains of root vegetables will need a lot of care and attention. Do we have the facilities and spare labour to support this? From my perspective of keeping people happy, I believe it is very important because food is a crucial feature of life on Mars.'

'I can see you think that,' said the AP, viewing the large pasta which Steve had ordered.

'Yes, well I hope you included ample stocks of penne pasta in the order or I'll be no use to you.'

'On that point, tomorrow, I might support the proposal in your report with two modifications. Firstly, you must explain what an allotment is because people from some countries will not appreciate that it is land divided up into small plots and allocated to those, often with no garden, who wish to cultivate them for flowers and vegetables. Secondly, to be efficient with the limited cultivation land available here, there must be some degree of collaborative cultivation. In other words, some can specialise in fruit, some on root vegetables, some on rice, some on green plants and maybe even some on… pasta plants.'

Steve smiled and responded, 'Some of these intensely focused astro-scientists here would probably believe your last example! But I see what you mean; maybe they could be specialist in one crop but still have a small area of their allotment for anything they liked.'

The AP agreed that could work. Steve offered to get him another Guinness, knowing full well that was beyond regulation levels, but he said he never normally had more than one and left. Later Steve did wonder about his use of the word *normally*.

Umbrella Thief

The rain it raineth on the just
And upon the unjust fella,
But more upon the just because
The unjust hath the just's umbrella.

SO RUNS THE ancient ditty, and usually that is the case, but not always. I well remember once when, complete with my briefcase and folding umbrella, I accepted a lift into Edinburgh with a colleague who was dropping off his car in the Gorgie area. I started to walk the remaining mile into the centre, but the rain clouds were gathering so I jumped on a bus. At the West End I alighted and had just started walking along Princes Street when large drops appeared, and it started raining in earnest. That was when I found I'd left my umbrella on the bus.

I had to look respectable and dry for the meeting I was to attend and was just beginning to panic when I noticed the bus I had been on moving slowly in the traffic queue beside me. I ran over and signalled to the driver but he just pointed to the next bus stop. I tried to explain by pointing to the back of the bus that I'd left something on it, but he seemed not to recognise me as a previous passenger and pointed more determinedly to the next bus stop. I grew frustrated with his misunderstanding and moved round to stand right in front of his bus so that he could not move while still gesticulating to convey my predicament. He then grudgingly opened the door, so I jumped on and explained. He then simply pointed towards the back with no comment, so I went to my previous seat to retrieve my umbrella.

A large lady with bulging shopping bags was in the seat but she kindly got up and helped me search and then an oldish man with a moustache who had been sitting behind joined in and even a skinny teenager shivering in his loose T-shirt and jeans. My umbrella, a rather good one actually, with stronger struts than normal and a polished wooden handle, was nowhere to be found.

'Someone's taken a fancy to it, ducky,' the large lady volunteered.

I searched the faces of those around for any signs of unease or guilt but to no avail. However, I noticed several folk had cases or polythene bags which could have partly hidden my umbrella with ease. By now the bus had reached Waverley railway station where I had to alight and as I prepared to venture forth into the pouring rain I glanced back. They were all sitting there, totally inscrutable and above all dry; in fact, the teenager's T-shirt had 'Super Dry' emblazoned on the front. But I knew one of them was in fact a common thief. Was it Mrs Shopping-Bags or Colonial Moustache or skinny Keven or some innocent-looking passenger a few seats away? Whoever it was, I hoped on first use the struts would spring out into a tangled web and rip it apart.

It was over a week later that I met the colleague who had given me the lift.

'I've been looking out for you,' he said. 'You left your umbrella in my car; do you want it back?'

I cringed and thought: I've been here before, got the wrong end of the stick and misconstrued the kindly human race or at least that part of it on the Number 66 bus that day. Perhaps the old ditty needs updating:

The rain it raineth on the wise
Also on forgetful fellas,
But less upon the wiser guys,
They know where they've left umbrellas.

Senior Customer Care

To Southern Gas Board 3rd September 2017
Sevenoaks Area.
Customer No. SO 478521

Dear Sir/Madam,
   I pay for my household gas monthly based on your estimate of my usage. Two months ago, I fell over and have been in hospital with a broken femur, consequently using no gas. I would be grateful if the last two payments could be refunded.
   Yours sincerely
   John Crawford.
   PS. I have no internet or email but do text on my mobile.

Dear Mr Crawford,
   Thank you for your letter of 3rd September. As stated in our Customer Care Policy (see www.southerngascare.co.uk), we only make corrections to estimated accounts annually when we read the meters. Unscheduled lack of usage during part of one year therefore will be automatically reflected in the payments made the following year. This allows us to reduce the costs to the benefit of all our customers.
   Yours faithfully,
   Molly Kingston
   Customer Care (Probationer).

Dear Ms Kingston,

I asked my daughter to visit your Southern Gas Office in Sevenoaks yesterday to obtain a copy of your Customer Care Policy. I note that it spells out your annual estimation and payment procedure but adds 'except where shorter terms are required'.

I am 98 years old and the wait of a year for correction of my overpayment represents nearly a third of my predicted remaining life according to insurance statistics. I consider waiting a third of my remaining life for the return of my payments to be a major injustice and I plan to complain to the government energy ombudsman forthwith.

Yours
Mr John Crawford.

Dear John

Thank you for your letter of 29th September. I do understand your concern regarding the delay at your advanced age as I did statistics in my final year at Uni before coming here last month. I showed your letter to my Customer Care Manager and he asked me to deal with it myself as he was too busy.

You will be pleased to know that I have arranged for your meter to be read next week after which your payments can be adjusted. I have also persuaded the nice folk in the meter reading team to contact you and have given them your mobile number.

With kind regards
Molly Kingston.
Customer Care (Probationer)

Transcript of voice exchange made for training purposes, 3.30pm on 3rd October, between the Meter Reading

Team and Customer No. SO 478521 on Mobile Phone 07763583640:

'Good afternoon, Mr Crawford. This is Sid from the Southern Gas Meter Unit. We understand you live at 16B Buckhurst Avenue.'

'Yes, that's correct, it's just behind Waitrose on the High Street.'

'Thank you, Mr Crawford, we know where Buckhurst Avenue is but cannot find No. 16B.'

'Yes, many people have that problem; it's along the alleyway between 15 and 17 and then you turn left.'

'Okay, thank you.'

Further exchange at 3.34pm (after a long tone ring):

'Mr Crawford, it's Sid again. I have found 16A and 16C but there's no B.'

'Oh, it's you again. Sorry about the delay in answering but I dropped the mobile. Yes, it's the brown door in the recess between the two. Actually, it does have a B on it below the handle you know but it's gone rusty and hardly shows. I keep meaning to paint it but the only brush I have has gone hard and the shop where I used to get brushes only sell lots on a plastic card rather than one at a time and...'

'That's fine, Mr Crawford, thank you.'

Further exchange at 3.37pm.

'Mr Crawford, it's Sid.'

'Yes,' (audible sigh) '... What is it this time?'

'We are now hammering on your door, 16B. Could you please come and open it?'

'No, I can't. As I explained in my letter to your people

at Southern Gas, I'm in hospital. I fell over and broke my femur two months ago and...'

'Oh bollocks!'

Click and out.

Email from the Manager, Customer Care Centre, Southern Gas to Novice Assistant, Molly Kingston, 8th October.

Molly,

I asked you to deal with costumer Mr J Crawford. His daughter has just telephoned me to complain about our treatment of him in respect of his current over-payment and also a related incident two days ago. Apparently one of our meter readers was rude to him and used a word he had not heard since his navy days. You were asked to deal with this customer so could you now issue him with our *Standard Apology for Senior Citizens* as set out in the staff guidelines issued to you at the commencement of your probation.

I would also like to bring your career assessment meeting forward to next Friday (7th October) at 4pm in order to discuss your continuing suitability for employment in this division of Southern Gas.

Manager, Customer Care Centre.

Lost in Translation

THE PEAT FIRE was smouldering reluctantly and Donegan gave it a wee poke which produced a few sparks. In midwinter the sun hardly rose above the horizon in this remote western corner of Iceland and the evenings were long and monotonous.

'Grandad, tell us again the saga of how you came to be here in Akranes and why you are not a Viking,' asked Magnus.

'Yes,' agreed Charlotta his sister, who at thirteen had heard the story more times than her very much younger brother, Magnus.

'Each time you tell us it's a little different.'

Donegan stroked his long rough beard. He knew they were angling to prolong the cosy warmth around the smoking peat before the long throes of the night but decided to oblige. He took a long draught of mead from his earthen jug, sat back and recited his story.

'I was born about the same time that our Thingvellir parliament was formed, 930 years after Christ, in far-away Ireland. I had a disease which left me barely able to walk for the rest of my life. My family knew I could never earn my keep so they offered me as a chattel to the nearby monastery. It so happened that over time the monks found I had a good head for learning and a good hand for illustrating their holy books in the Bible.'

He settled back in the cosy fur of his makeshift chair. He loved telling this story.

'One day some of them went on a pilgrimage to the Northern Isles and the Abbot asked me to go and help them converse with the barbarians of those parts. Apart from being good at picking up other languages I was lame and thus no threat to the expedition leaders. After a long voyage and a storm where we nearly perished, we settled here owing to the natural harbour. There was a small hamlet of Vikings from Norway and they were initially tolerant of this band of monks in their long cassocks, having come themselves only a few score of years before.

'The monks then built themselves a rough wooden shelter large enough to accommodate them all at the harbour by cutting down some of the trees growing on the small island we can see just off the coast and floating the logs across. This upset the Viking village folk and they argued with the monks about using up the trees because there were very few around. When I say argued, I mean gesticulated and shouted because the Vikings spoke their language, a variant of Norse, and the monks their native Irish. I managed to learn Norse with the help of a comely fair-headed girl who was the daughter of their leader. The monks were envious of this association because they had taken a vow of celibacy.'

'What does celibacy mean?' piped up Magnus.

'It means they can't shag women,' ventured Charlotta.

'Charlotta, don't talk like that. At thirteen you're not meant to know about such things, and your mother and grandmother would be shocked. I'd get a rollicking too.'

'Thirteen and three quarters,' corrected Charlotta. Magnus said nothing, so Donegan carried on.

'I explained to the Vikings as best I could that the monks were holy men needing proper shelter for the coming winter and did not know how to build turf huts like the Vikings. It all came to a head over food rather than accommodation a few months later. The monks had built their shelter near the harbour, which meant they had easy access to the fish, while the Vikings had moved a little inland in order to grow vegetables. But vegetables are seasonal and fish are not, so fish became of key importance in the winter.

'The monks were getting up very early and using an ancient method of immersing their hands under the water, tickling the fish and flipping them out. The Vikings arose earlier and earlier but the monks were always there before them. The Vikings remonstrated with the monks but finally they had had enough. One morning the men of the village, led by their Viking chief, donned their battle outfits, grabbed their scabbards and shields and insisted that the monks leave immediately, once and for all. By then my appreciation of their language had greatly improved and I knew that the word they used for 'insisted' meant immediately, then and there, or they would tear the monks limb from limb and throw them in the harbour.'

'Then they would have no arms or legs to swim with,' ventured Magnus excitedly.

'Stupid,' muttered Charlotta, nudging her brother in the side.

'Once again, I explained to the angry men of the village that the monks were holy men and so rose up early to pray rather than to fish. But this was to no avail and indeed the Vikings extended the disembowelling to removal of their, er, genitals.'

'Mind your language, Grandad,' chimed in Charlotta impertinently with a grin.

'They insisted I accurately inform the monks of their pending fate, as that was only just and fair; Vikings are an honourable people. But I knew the monks too well and guessed they would view this as a trial of their faith from

God and thus resist at all costs. I also knew it would lead to them all perishing horribly at the hands of the Vikings. So, I translated the message constructively in the interests of peace and told them that the Vikings were warning about the great volcano in the distance beyond the hot geysers, how it was about to erupt and that they must move away immediately or die. I said the Vikings were already packed and ready to go (to explain the battle dress).

'On cue, the faithful geyser let forth one of its mightiest spurts of scalding water high into the firmament. Maybe the gods were on my side and this was their sign. The monks, after a quick confab, decided to flee by boat back to Ireland. I negotiated a day's grace to allow them time to pack their possessions and make their boat seaworthy. Peace-making is arduous and well deserves the awarded biblical blessing. At the last moment as they were leaving, the Viking chief insisted that I remain with them as a hostage to ensure the monks left with no trouble. I was obviously unhappy about this but the monks promised they would one day return to collect me.

'I was very sad for a long time and every morning looked forlornly out over the southern seas. However, the Vikings were very kind to me, especially the girl I had met. I taught them many things about foreign lands and she taught me many things about the ways of the Vikings. Gradually over the years, as my memory of the lush green countryside of Ireland faded, I became one among them. As you know, I now even represent the Akranes area in the Thingvellir, which is why our Parliament has a solitary Irish member.

'I never saw the monks again but a few years ago I did hear a tale from an Irish skipper about a group of Irish missionaries who went to convert these parts and how their God warned them of a great volcano that was about to erupt and they were all saved. I've never thought of myself as a god before but if the cap fits, I'll wear it.

'Now you two, off you go to your bunks.'

Magnus had dozed off but Charlotta had a burning question.

Was our gran the daughter of their chief?'

'Yes, that's right, Charlotta.'

She looked thoughtful for a moment.

'Do you think she persuaded her father, the Viking chief, to take you as a hostage when they chased the monks away?'

'Off you go to bed now,' said Donegan, getting up to show he meant it.

Forgotten but not Gone

IN THE LITTLE village that is home to the first few hundred voyagers on planet Mars, a disaster struck. The same had happened on Earth 400 years before in the first American colonies. It started with one of the Terminauts, Shane, suffering from what the two resident doctors thought was just a bad cold. Shane, an Australian who had made his millions in sheep farming at the turn of the millennium, had already had serious prostate cancer and thought he would like to leave the earth in style. In spite of pleading from his family to stay with them, if not in spirit at least in body (correct way round) he nevertheless pursued his wish to die on Mars. Once there he started to enjoy his grumpy old man status and decided to delay the reason for going as long as possible. After all, he had paid eight million dollars to join this happy band of Terminauts. He was thus not best pleased when some deadly Martian flu took hold of him just when he was beginning to enjoy himself.

Rev Steve McKay, the village chaplain, had only been on Mars for six months and was finding the transfer from a leafy parish in Scotland to these concrete domes in the regolith totally disconcerting. However, visiting the ill and dying was well part of his training and he set about it with fortitude. Shane had serious respiratory issues four nights later and was showing a steady decline, so Steve went to see him and administer what comfort he could. Steve, like others caring for the infected patients, had to don a white hazmat suit which made him look particularly foreboding. Shane was not religious and assumed Steve was simply seeing him as part of his round; he was, after all, the chaplain. However, on his second visit within 24 hours, Shane perceived that Steve was performing an extra duty or even administering the last rites and this made him even less happy.

'Might have guessed that some Pommy bastard in a white coat would turn up when I'm really down to earn himself a kudos point,' he growled.

Steve stared at the gaunt man lying there with a mix of sympathy and annoyance.

'I'm Scottish so not strictly Pommy; and I'm not a bastard, I'm the chaplain,' said Steve stiffly.

'You're probably both,' retorted the frail voice.

'And what are you, then?' said Steve.

'I was the biggest sheep farmer in Western Australia.'

'Well, you're not the biggest sheep farmer now,' said Steve as he looked down on the emaciated frame in the bed.

Shane opened his eyes – they had been almost closed – and peered at Steve for a moment with interest.

'Thought you guys were meant to be all sweetness and light.'

'We are, but not to crusty old sheep farmers even if they did own half of Australia,' said Steve.

'So, what happens to me now? I've cashed in my fortune for a last trip to Mars (which really upset the hangers-on) only to die of some dreaded flu in this God-forsaken planet.'

'Well, it's not God-forsaken because God loves Mars too –', but Shane cut him off.

'No, I don't want all that religious stuff, I want to know what happens to *me*. They can't bury me owing to contamination, they can't eject me into space as it's too expensive and they can't cremate me because there's no bloody oxygen so what happens to me; this me here?'

Steve paused for a moment before admitting:

'I really don't know.'

'Well, that's a first,' said Shane. 'A chaplain who doesn't know what happens to you when you go. I suppose at least that's honest.'

'I'll speak to the Mars Council and let you know,' said Steve, feeling somewhat inadequate. He stared at the floor, thinking, but was summarily dismissed.

'Well get the hell out of here and find out then, or I'll be gone without knowing,' complained Shane.

It was two days later that Steve tracked down the Council member responsible among other things for disposal of waste products. Apparently, it was exactly as Shane had said: the body issue had been shelved, literally, by agreeing to place them in a concrete sarcophagus stored in a concrete mausoleum where they would not decay for 100 years in the Mars environment. Among Mars folk, translation error or whatever transposed 'Mausoleum' into 'Marsoleum', and so Marsoleum it became. Steve felt a little miffed that, as chaplain, he had neither been consulted nor informed.

The next day when he revisited Shane, he duly informed him.

'You mean to say I'll have my own temple on Mars?' he whispered, having now become very weak.

'Not quite,' said Steve, 'because it will have to be shared with Fred who's already been cold stored for a couple of months and any others that come along. But you'll be in the Marsoleum for 100 years and will have your name inscribed on the front, or the side, with an appropriate inscription of up to 20 letters – for any passers-by to read!'

He was not quite sure why he added this; sometimes things just come out in spite of yourself; even to a dying man.

To Steve's consternation Shane started to shake a little and it took Steve a moment to realise that actually he was laughing.

'How about… "I'm on the other side." Is that less than 20 letters?'

He then added:

'You realise I'll have left the Earth without dying. I'll be like Elisha: he left the Earth without dying, didn't he?'

'You're right,' said Steve, somewhat taken aback, 'but how do you know about that?'

'Us farmers in the Outback all went to Sunday School; we know a thing or two about these things; it's not just you chaplain types with all your learning. I want to die out here in space because I'll be halfway there.'

'Yes, I know, I understand and you're right, it's all a journey and Earth's just a stop en route; and no, you haven't lost your way, you're right on target.'

'Thank you, Chaplain, much appreciated. Now bugger off as I've become tired and want to sleep with my thoughts.'

'And what's the inscription to be?'

Steve lent over and just heard Shane whisper:

'Forgotten but not Gone.'

Rock of Ages

IT WAS A day that Jenny would never forget, nor for that matter would all those folk of East Lothian who lived through it. She lived in a cottage to the north of Traprain, that great igneous rock that protrudes from the rolling hills of the green countryside like a surfacing whale.

Its formation long ago was also reminiscent of a surfacing whale as a great swath of molten lava broke through the thin crust of the earth at this point, forcing its way between the sedimentary rocks to form a rare laccolith intrusion. Three hundred million years of erosion had left the massive dome exposed, but the crust around it remained thinner and more fractured than before. The earth's thin crust is only a few miles thick in places and can be gradually eroded on the inside by movement of the hot viscous magma underneath. It is rather like pastry crust above a steak pie bubbling away in the oven while being cooked. Furthermore, environmental warming had also altered the global cooling patterns that contribute to the delicate thermal balance keeping this crust as we know it. Deep measurements by geologists had indicated hot spots in fragile areas around these laccoliths, including this prominent example in the middle of East Lothian.

Jenny, though, knew very little about all this. To her it was merely a friendly giant behind her cottage. On sunny mornings like this, when long morning shadows were cast over the fields, it represented something enduring and solid in a confusing world, a rock of ages.

Early on that fateful morning, as Jenny left the cottage to walk along the track by the field, she noticed that Archie, her chestnut Spaniel, hung around rather than bouncing off. At first, she thought that he might be poorly or had seen Doreen's horrible Alsatian across the field; indeed, he seemed to be furtively looking back now and then.

She then felt a slight vibration and thought it was something amiss with herself until she saw the birds flying in tight circles above, squawking as if warning of a nearby sparrow hawk. There it was again, a distinct rumble and then another rumble, way below the ground. Then beside the track she saw a gap open up and steamy mist rise from it. Wide-eyed disbelief translated into gut reaction and both Jenny and Archie turned and ran off down the track away from Traprain as fast as they could.

Five minutes later, as she rushed down towards the ruined castle at Hailes, she saw old Joe outside his farm cottage.

'Joe, Joe,' she puffed, 'get out of here, the Rock is melting and hissing steam and we'll all be burnt alive, come on…'

He just stared at her with that sympathetic, patronising look she had got used to from the locals who thought of her as eccentric and even slightly backward. Maybe she was; had she really seen all this? She paused for a moment and looked back towards Traprain, her mighty rock on which all her security was grounded. It was now surrounded by steam and, horror upon horror, she could just see the surface of molten red sludge at the base which illuminated it with a reddish glow. The ground rumbled again, so she turned and ran and ran until she reached the River Tyne. The footbridge had collapsed, so she waded across to the opposite bank and sat down exhausted with Archie panting at her side.

Jenny reviewed her position. She had heard this was a

volcanic area in a school lesson long ago and realised there was now a great disaster unfolding before her very eyes. She must warn folk about it in case they had not heard, but how? Her mobile was still in her cottage and possibly melting in the lava by now. She decided to carry on up the north bank of the Tyne towards the A1 main road at the top.

The initial eruption must have started much earlier because the A1 was already busy with cars and fire engines and ambulances rushing about, so she slumped down on the verge. Archie, whom she held tightly on his lead, was agitated. He snuggled up to her and started to whimper, which in turn made her cry. She could see the whole area that had been home for so long lying in the direct path of the dark red sludge oozing out from under Traprain and prayed that the folk living nearby had managed to escape. Traprain itself, no longer an immobile rock, appeared to be floating on the ash and lava surrounding it. She was mesmerised and shocked that this could happen so suddenly in southern Scotland. It should be in Italy or Iceland or somewhere else, not here among our lush rolling hills that had always seemed so steadfast and sure.

A car pulled up onto the verge beside her and the driver wound down the passenger window.

'You can't stay there, lass, the air will soon be laden with ash and it's not safe beside the motorway.'

'I've run up from beside Traprain where I live, there's quite a few people living down there in the Tyne valley.'

'Yes, there're are all being evacuated – I've just heard it on the radio. If you jump in, I'll drop you off in Musselburgh where they are setting up a disaster centre. I'm a retired doctor going there to see if I can help… And bring that dog, it looks even more shocked than you.'

She climbed in beside him, pinching herself to make sure this was not a dream.

The old church in the High Street had been opened that morning as one of the disaster hubs and people were flocking there from the east. Police, council workers, medical folk and others were helping many who were shell-shocked and disorientated. Resilience committees had on occasions in the past discussed disaster management but this was totally beyond anything they had envisaged, so people were falling back on their own resources.

Jenny held Archie close beside her. She felt sorry for these people in the hub and quickly started assisting where she could. Somebody in authority trying to organise things asked her to help those needing physical assistance and she set to, pushing wheelchairs and getting tea for folk. By late afternoon she was exhausted and sat down for a break herself. Those around were appreciative, chatting with her about their experiences, and they loved her dog who just could not believe all the attention he was getting. For the first time Jenny felt part of it all and truly normal like others, not just 'poor Jenny' as the locals thought of her.

That night they made up makeshift beds on the church floor from donated mattresses and bedding and Archie, who thought it was all for him, settled on one of them. Lying there, Jenny realised something for the first time. She had escaped from under the shadow of that great rock and those local folk, some of whom had made her feel so awkward and ineffective. She decided she would not return to the area after it all cooled down, even if it was possible. This was partly because it would never be the same and partly owing to a touch of guilt: this terrible disaster for so many had, for her, occasioned a revelation.

Final Adjustments

MY AVERSION TO forever making final adjustments once led to me starting the oldest *motor car* in the world. It was the Autumn of 1999, I believe, when I was attending the Eurotherm meeting in Heidelberg as one of two UK representatives. The purpose was to plan the next series of Eurotherm conferences when the EC scientists and engineers like myself, involved with heat transfer and heat exchangers, could meet up to present academic papers and swap their know-how. Some cynics used to refer to them as Euro-jollies but, while accepting that essential refreshments were considered a welcome catalyst, they did wonders for international co-operation. The key plans and dates for the next couple of years were established on the first day, so the next day was spent on final adjustments, something that many engineers find pretty exciting. This seemed a good time to make myself scarce, especially when there was a great attraction only 50 miles away. This was the renowned Mercedes-Benz Museum at the Daimler factory in Stuttgart, the very heart of motoring history.

And so it was that I emerged from Stuttgart railway station one blustery November afternoon and made my way to the museum. Unlike most museums, you were at that time taken on a guided tour rather than meandering around between the exhibits. The tour lasted about an hour and a description in perfect English of each exotic car was given in glowing terms by the guide. As an engineer I wanted to examine some of the cars in more detail but was dragged along with the crowd. One in particular, the first real car ever, a three-wheeled Benz, was of especial interest to me. Consequently, when the tour finished and the next tour group brushed by us, I slipped unnoticed to join them and had a repeat performance. At least, I thought it was unnoticed but I was approached by a smartly dressed official towards the end who commented that I must be especially keen on their cars, so I quickly explained my particular interest in the early Benz. He said:

'Well, it's your lucky day because once a month we start the car to keep it functional and you can give me a hand.'

Whereupon he led me back to car with its spindly wire wheels and primitive horizontal engine mounted above the rear axle. He showed me how to start it by swinging the large horizontal flywheel and within a few moments the single cylinder spluttered into life and settled down to a steady *phut, phut, phut*... I had started the oldest car in the world. (The Museum has since been rehoused in a beautiful double-helix building and I suspect that display protocol and security would disallow such an experience these days.)

'So why were you so fascinated by this car?' he asked.

'It's not so much the car,' I explained, 'as the circumstances of its first journey.'

I should perhaps explain to those poor folk who manage to drift through life unaware of the fascinating history and heritage of the vintage motorcar, that Herr Carl Benz, working in Mannheim in 1885, had almost perfected his first *Motorwagen*. Almost but not quite. His long-suffering wife, Bertha, and teenage boys, Eugen and Richard, had witnessed the man of the house tinkering with his new-fangled device in his workshop every evening for over three years. In defence of his obsession, he had explained that one day it would be finished and he would take the family to see her mother in Pforzheim, nearly 70 kilometres away – a sop to win her forbearance if ever. By 1888, Bertha had had enough. Early one morning, with the support of her boys, she silently wheeled the motor out of the workshop to a distance beyond earshot of the sleeping Carl and managed to start it. The three of them mounted the ungainly contraption and set off over muddy tracks and roughly cobbled roads towards Pforzheim. The journey took 12 hours and included many adventures, including cleaning of the carburettor with a hat-feather, using her garter as a fan belt and hard bargaining in chemists' shops to obtain the ligoin cleaning agent as fuel.

'Hi Mum, it's me' (or its nineteenth-century German equivalent) was met with incredulity that this iron cart, with a noisy piston arrangement instead of a horse, had travelled through all the villages and towns from Mannheim. The journey is well recorded in the motoring annals for those who want more. Carl was less than happy when he received her telegram that evening as he still had not made the final adjustments.

My guide, who had so kindly let me get my hands on the most celebrated car in the world, turned out to be a Director of the Museum. In our subsequent chat over coffee, he returned to my initial interest in the car with the observation:

'I suppose it demonstrates how the search for mechanical perfection by a genius engineer can overcome the most daunting of hurdles.'

'Yes, but if it had not been for Bertha's exasperation, he might have been forever making final adjustments to attain that perfection,' I ventured. 'And in the meantime, the French or even the British might have stolen a march!'

'Maybe,' he grinned, 'but they were a long way behind

and actually she did not do most of the driving: it was Eugen, who was only 15 at the time. She spent the journey fettling the mixture controls and planning the route to chemists' shops, avoiding the worst hills. So, Eugen was the first long-distance driver or alternatively teenage joy-rider. Most accounts don't mention that in case the local teenagers try to emulate his achievement.'

We parted with a handshake at the entrance, and I made my way back to Heidelberg with a warm feeling of achievement. Meanwhile, they were still making final adjustments to the Eurotherm programme until mid-evening and had hardly noticed my absence,

I would like to have told you more about Bertha Benz and how she championed the horseless carriage right up until she died in 1944 at the age of 95. Her journey is celebrated today by veteran runs along the same route, and so on.

[Apologies, but there's no time for all that as I'm up against a deadline. This write-up has to be submitted to my writing group tonight. But what about all those infringements of grammar and syntax errors and sentences like this starting and even finishing with 'but'. Too late, I'm afraid; it's going off without the final adjustments.]

Abandoned Practice

'WE'LL TRY THAT hymn chorus again with a slightly longer pause at the end of each line to add emphasis,' insisted Jill, the pretty choir mistress of St John's.

They started singing once more: –

> 'All things bright and beautiful,' (pause)
> 'All creatures great and small,' (pause)
> 'All things wise and wonderful,'

But Fred, the bearded organist, had rendered no pause as requested and was out of sync. Had he not heard?

'Stop, stop,' shouted Jill. 'Fred, can we have a little longer at the end of the lines?'

'It's not musically correct to do that. It spoils the flow, so I'd rather not,' responded Fred.

Jill bristled at this challenge to her authority in front of the choir. He did it practically every week. She reddened and said matter-of-factly,

'I'm the choir mistress here and that's the way I'd like it – they need a breath between these lines, you know. The instrument is an accompaniment to the singing, not the other way round.'

He responded crossly, 'I'm the organist and I play what's written, not what a chorister thinks it should be.'

She was livid: she was the choir mistress, not just a chorister and as such the leader, the one to be obeyed. She stomped over to where Fred was perched on his organist's stool and stamped her foot hard on the floor. However, it caught against the lowest bass foot pedal board and struck a note which duly responded with a gravelly roar reverberating throughout the old church. It sounded to her like the guffaws of some distant fiend.

'That's it, I've had enough,' she fumed. 'I and my choir are off; you can sit here and play with yourself all night.'

She realised she could have put it better, but on the other hand…

The dumb-struck choir duly abandoned their practice and traipsed out with her. They all filed into the White Hart across the road and ordered pints and proseccos and things. The rest of the evening was enjoyed by all and there was no mention of the affray.

Later Jill walked the few hundred yards home to find her husband watching the 10 o'clock news. She settled down in a chair nearby and said not a word. In the middle of a TV interview of some Brexit pundit he said:

'We really should not have so many domestics in front of the choir, you know: they'll think we're dysfunctional.'

Senorita de Mister

HER REAL NAME was Sally Black. She was the wife of the chairman of the local Alvis Club, not to be confused with the Elvis club. The Alvis Classic Car Club is dedicated to the memory and maintenance of Alvis cars made by the British company from 1921 to 1967. The chairman loved his two exotic Alvis cars with an ardour that only the most dedicated of technocrats can muster, and Sally had long ago resigned herself to merely a supportive role in third place behind the cars.

At club gatherings in the grounds of select country hotels, he would either arrive in goggles and leather cap abreast his 1931 open sporting 12/50 model or in his 1936 Charlesworth Speed 20 Saloon with its long bonnet, enormous chrome headlights and sumptuous leather interior. Both were the envy of club members, and Sally would dutifully help polish the woodwork, clean the windows and assist with connolising the rich soft brown leather. He usually took the Speed 20 Saloon to the events and on long journeys Sally undertook the navigation as he was not into maps and wouldn't allow SatNav devices in such a period masterpiece. She was also allocated the duty of clearing the inside of the windscreen which, as in all old cars with limited ventilation, constantly misted up. So, with a map on her knees and a damp cloth in her hand she suffered many a mile within the confines of walnut panelling and soft brown leather.

He was not totally unappreciative of her assistant's role

and occasionally introduced her to new members while discussing their cars. It was always the same:

'This is my wife, Senorita de Mister,' followed by a chuckle as he explained that her primary duty was as his windscreen demister.

The new member would laugh politely, and Sally would smile weakly. Maybe the first time it was funny but by the twentieth it was wearisome although she bore her supportive role with dignity.

The day came for the National Event, this time held in a stately home in the Highlands. It attracted hundreds of members with scores of Alvises and our chairman was keen to exhibit both of his cars on such a prestigious occasion, but that would require another driver. As it happened there was an Alvis member named Bob living nearby, but he only drove a TA14. The TA14 was a rather undistinguished Alvis model produced just after the War when component supplies were difficult to obtain, and the chairman had little truck with him. However, needs must, and he contacted Bob who readily agreed to drive the Charlesworth Speed 20 to the event. This also had the advantage of preventing Bob taking his own inferior Alvis to such an important gathering.

On the appointed day Bob parked his TA14 by the chairman's house and settled himself into the driver's seat of the Speed 20. After many instructions on driving it from the chairman he was surprised by Sally who jumped into the passenger seat, explaining that she was not going in the 12/50 as it had no hood and no windscreen. It was a long drive and Bob was grateful that he had a navigator and that every five minutes or so she leant across to clear the windscreen as the weather was muggy and dull. After a couple of hours along a meandering route proscribed by the Club he suggested:

'What about stopping for a coffee if we can find somewhere?'

'Well,' she answered, 'I took the liberty of packing a few sandwiches and a flask.'

It was his second surprise of the day. He pulled off down a tract and parked with a view of the countryside behind a tall hedge.

Old cars have restricted front seats while the back seats have polished wood picnic trays which fold down for this very purpose, so they made themselves comfortable in the luxurious back sofa seat with its recently connolised leather and a central armrest. After consuming layers of beef and mustard accompanied by little bottles of red wine discovered in a side pocket, they were feeing pleasantly jovial and, having a sweet tooth, he said:

'What have you got for afters?'

She knew he had asked innocently and just for the joke nestled up close to him laughing. He laughed too and, not to appear prudish, he put his arm around her. It was hot in the car, and she undid the top button of her blouse. He undid the next one and it all seem to flow from there along a path of its own. At some point the central armrest was raised and a good time was had by all. That was his third surprise of the day.

Half an hour later the car was still misted up and, as they moved off to continue the journey, she leaned across to demist the windscreen once more. They arrived rather late, and the chairman was not best pleased as he directed them into his special space near the front of the display.

'Surely Bob you could have hurried; it is, after all, a Speed 20, not your sluggish old TA14.' But Bob just smiled and said nothing.

In the course of inspecting the car to ensure it was all neat and tidy, the chairman noticed that, oddly, the back armrest was up and he lowered it to its correct position. On witnessing this, Sally felt just a tinge of discomfort but it quickly evaporated as he introduced her to yet another Alvis club member,

'This is my wife, Senorita de Mister.'

Sailing Club

BIG BERT JONES had been a model prisoner and after five years, followed by a period on observed parole, he was released. It was difficult to believe this gentle giant of a man had once been so violent.

He had worked in an old-fashioned foundry making small batches of aluminium sand castings for local industries. It was hot, sweaty, manual work in the moulding section, making casts and breaking the sand after the metal had solidified and cooled. There were two of them working each shift and they were expected to work together as a team, but Bert could not take to Jack, the person with him. Jack was shifty and avoided pulling his weight, which was bad enough but it was the occasional snide remarks that really caused offence. Over a period of months Bert developed an intense dislike of Jack which fermented into irrational hatred, and he had difficulty restraining himself from lashing out on several occasions.

It came to a head when Jack noticed that Bert was often seen around with a young boy. He was unaware that Bert had a son following a liaison about ten years before and while Bert and the mother had long since separated, he still took the boy out on occasions. One morning, a heated exchange over the movement of mould cases became increasingly acrimonious and personal in the stifling heat of the foundry until Jack called Bert a bloody pervert. This unsurprisingly tipped Bert over the edge and he landed a solid right-hand punch on Jack which sent him sprawling across the foundry. Jack tripped at the edge of a large crucible of molten aluminium, pawed in the air in a desperate attempt to keep his balance, but lost it and fell in. They say his screams could be heard all over the town but were mercifully short-lived.

The initial consideration of a murder charge was commuted to aggravated manslaughter but nevertheless Bert found himself with an eight-year prison sentence. Following his release, three years early but under close scrutiny from probation officers, he could only find a job as a part-time hotel porter. He became increasingly dejected when he realised a reputation for violence would be indelibly inscribed on his record. He wondered if such a tendency was also embedded deep within him, some genetic abnormality that would forever thwart his wish to be like others.

One sunny afternoon he was wandering through a park near Eastleigh in Hampshire. It had a narrow-gauge train circuit on which real steam trains were puffing along hauling a gaggle of parents and excited children. It was somewhat contrived but it did produce whiffs of oily steam which reminded Bert of his youthful past. Further along there was a small lake with ducks and the most beautiful model sailing boats he had ever seen. The yachts, about three feet high with gleaming white sails, were being expertly manoeuvred by half a dozen folk with remote controllers. He sat down on a bench nearby and watched, fascinated by their expertise at sailing the model yachts round a small island and managing to avoid one and other in spite of the gentle wind changes. One of the men noticed Bert's fascination and came across to speak with him. He showed him the controls and chatted about the yachts, eventually asking him if he would like a shot. Bert was unused to this casual kindness but his desire overcame his reluctance and he found himself in control of a most exquisite sailing vessel. He loved it and found that he was a natural sailor, steering it expertly using the hand-held remote controller around obstructions including an inquisitive duck. The men were impressed and asked him to join them at the same time the following week.

Over the next few months he was there whenever they met and they duly invited him to join their Sailing Club. He purchased on eBay an old model yacht made of wood which happened to have a powerful electric motor driving a propeller in addition to its sails. He assured the club he would never use the motor as it was a sailing club. On occasions they had competitive sailing races around the island with the winner having a free round in the Red Dragon where they inevitably ended up. Bert was settling down to having a group of friends who knew nothing of his background and took him at face value. One of them, though, they called him Reg, would niggle him occasionally about being the new boy or comment on the way he sailed his old wooden boat. At least his boat had real wood on the deck, albeit a little worn, rather than plastic coating and in any case the others said they rather liked it. Reg made disparaging remarks about the other club members too but whereas they seemed to just ignore him, Bert developed a real and rather disproportionate dislike of him. Living on his own and having time to brood did not help and it all came to a head one evening when they were practising formation sailing in preparation for a fête the following Saturday.

As they were rounding the island Reg steered his large and magnificent blue yacht into the side of Burt's wooden sailing boat just enough to send it slight off course towards the bank. Burt knew that this was not accidental.

'Your wooden ark is too primitive for these events,' Reg shouted across to him with a sneering look.

Burt was furious. His neck reddened and he clenched his fists. His boat was by now four feet behind Reg's yacht. He activated the banned electric motor on his boat and it surged ahead like a speed boat, catching the yacht on the inside as it made a turn. The impact was enough to tip Reg's posh sailing yacht over so that the sail lay in the water. Unfortunately, it had also dislodged the balance weight at the base of the keel so that it did not right itself. He had landed a nautical killer punch which not only shocked himself but even more so Reg, who took to swearing at him profusely. To add insult to injury, a Mallard duck swam over and pecked the wet sail.

Bert quickly recovered his composure and steered his boat to nudge Reg's stricken yacht to the bank where he recovered it for him while apologising. He offered to pay for any damage, which could have been considerable as the electronics was soaking wet too, but Reg grabbed it from him and strode off in a temper while the others stood around witnessing the scene with mounting apprehension.

'Time to go to the pub,' one of them suggested.

He looked at Bert who was standing there looking totally lost.

'You too,' he added as they went off.

Bert did not go but sat there on the bench by himself. So, the gremlin in his make-up was still there. He could still conjure up an intense dislike from nothing much for a certain type of person. He could still go that step further than required. Maybe he was not, and never would be, quite like others. A dark cloud that he hoped had gone was still there on the horizon to darken his existence. At that moment he was totally drained and empty. He should just go home and not return, ever.

He sat there for some time.

No, he made a decision. He was going to fight it, not give way to such moods. He arose and determinedly strode off to the pub where he knew they would be seated around the ancient table in the corner thinking about the incident and probably discussing how he had flipped. He would join them and try to explain. Maybe he would have to disclose his past but be that as it may.

He strode in. They were sitting there as expected. The seat he normally used nearest to the door was invitingly pulled back a little. On the table they had placed his usual pint of London Pride. He sat down and took a sip, just about holding himself together. The guy who had first welcomed him all those months ago said:

'The sod has texted us to say he's resigned from the Sailing Club. All of us have felt like killing him at various times but you did the next best thing. Proves you're one of us.'

'Doesn't let you off buying the next round though,' he added.

Mum's Church

Class 3B Exercise – Write a 1000-word essay on your mum.

My mum's all upset. I could tell because she looked grumpy and only gave me beans on toast with no egg on the top for my tea. I tried to cheer her up by telling her about my good mark in mathematics that day. Mathematics is a great subject because it deals with facts and truth and is not spoilt by the mushy views of the teachers. I'm pretty good with figures and the Internet and all that. *(In fact, I've got this very essay on Google word count so I know how much more I've got to write and can stop when I get to 1000!)*

Once upset, Mum can stay like that for several days, so I decided to have it out with her, face to face.

'Mum, why are you looking like death warmed up; has Dad contacted you or have we run out of money again before the end of the month or something?'

I should explain Dad works in the Royal Bank and he went off with sleazy Amanda from Customer Services about a year ago but the loser still loiters around and rings us up to make trouble.

'No, it's nothing you need concern yourself with, Adrian.' But her glance fell on the kirk magazine, and I knew it was her church making her unhappy, so I just picked it up and waited.

'Well, okay, you might as well know, they are going to close our village kirk when Rev MacMillan retires because 121 can't afford to pay for a new minister.'

I should explain to the great unchurched that apparently 121 is some grand stone edifice in George Street, Edinburgh, that runs the Church of Scotland. It seems they can close village kirks willy-nilly, but then I'm only 13 and three-quarters so may have got it wrong. Mind you, only a few old people go any rate so it's no big deal, but if it's upset my mum then I'm on to it.

Mum used to take me to Sunday School when I was a kid and I would have to sit at the front with the others and listen to Bible stories. They were all posh kids with Nike trainers and flashy new bikes and two parents. I mean, what do you want two parents for? One's as much as I can manage. The minister would always ask us questions to entertain the congregation. I never quite gave him the blindingly obvious answer he wanted so eventually he stopped asking me in favour of that know-all Gerald who wore his school jacket even on Sundays. *(417 words, long way to go.)*

'But Mum, why can't they afford a minister? You and all the other old people pay every week. I saw you pay a ten-pound note once and then we ran out of money by Friday and had to have fish and chips with no fish.'

'Adrian, you don't understand, the Church is poor because so few people go and they do give some money away to third-world countries and refugees.'

'There you go again, Mum, it's always that I don't understand. I'm not stupid, you know, just because I'm about 100 years younger than you. I'm going to go and look on the Internet right now. I might even ask Dad, so there. At least he knows about money and accounts and things, even if he is a tosser.'

'No, please don't speak to Dad, it'll just cause trouble,' but by then I was determinedly on my way upstairs to my own computer screen in my own bedroom.

After some surfing, I found annual accounts for the

whole Church of Scotland for 2020 – they were a little hidden away in the depth of the net but I'm pretty good at finding things. I could be a really good hacker if I wanted. Apparently, their total worth is, phew, £743 million pounds. Seems that much of it is in buildings and tied up with salaries and running costs but there's over £150 million of it in investments and accounts which can be spent.

I texted Dad who seemed a bit surprised I'd contacted him and he asked why I wanted to know about this. I texted a quick explanation and he looked it up and replied that the Church was indeed one of the richest groups in Scotland and, yes, £150 million was deposits and spendable investments with lots more in buildings that could be sold.

So, I went back downstairs to Mum who was looking very sad and told her they had over £150 million to spend if they wished. I reckoned they should be paying her back each week for all that money she's donated. Or, as I worked out in my head, they could pay 100 new ministers £50,000 a year for the next 20 years and still have enough change for their pensions.

She said nothing for some time and I wondered if I'd got my sums wrong, but then, looking down, she muttered to herself:

'Maybe they think it's their money like the banks do, and when the rainy day comes, they can decide to keep it for an even more rainy day.'

She then looked up at me and said:

'They tell us nothing about all this on Sunday and how the Church can be saved but only talk about those poor people 2000 years ago.'

I piped up with: 'But they weren't all poor. There was that very rich man 2000 years ago who, just like the

Church, asked how he could be saved. What was he told to do?'

Mum said, 'He was told to go and sell all his possessions and give the money to the poor. We are told his face fell and he went away sad because he had many possessions.'

'Maybe that's why the Church is sad,' I suggested.

She smiled; I was so pleased it was all fine again. She never mentioned the matter after that. On sunny Sundays she began taking me out instead of going to that church all the time and we had eggs on our beans on toast and fish with our fish and chips… *(that's the end, over 1000 words, yippee)*

Running into Trouble

I KNEW IT was wrong to start writing a short story while watching the England-France Six-Nations 2021 rugby game at the same time. But then we are designed to do two things at once; after all, we have two ears to hear two conversations, two eyes to see things, two hands and so on. Presumably we have only one mouth to stop us arguing with ourselves.

Wow, they've only just kicked off and Dupont has already scored a try for France after one minute, that must be a record surely, and it's converted too, to give a them early lead of seven points.

As a teenager I was only just over 10 stone but I did play rugby for my school because I was a very fast runner. In those days it was standard practice to place runners on the wings and although I was pretty poor at rugby or any competitive ball game, I could certainly run. It was pretty boring on the wing most of the time and your mind could drift from the game in hand but I do remember once when the ball arrived from nowhere and I just ran and ran with it. They were all shouting and I assumed it was encouragement until I noticed they were all pointing too. With horror I realised I was going towards the wrong end so I did a quick U-turn and charged all the way back. This manoeuvre took them and not least the ref completely by surprise and in the disarray, I scored them a try. I later argued forcefully it was an intended ploy.

That's England now with their own try, borne of righteous indignation at their opponents gaining a lead while they were warming up. Farrell has converted so it's an equal score, that's better.

How these guys manage to kick like that always amazes me, having virtually no hand-eye or leg-eye co-ordination. That's the thing about running, it needs no skill whatsoever; you just look at the horizon and go for it. It's really an apology for sport – I used to love it, even ran for Buckinghamshire County Under-16s when I could do half a mile in a tad over two minutes. It was useful too, once, when…

Now England has picked up no less than two successful penalty kicks, giving them a 13-7 lead. Not sure what caused the second penalty, I should concentrate more. I'll get another bottle of Belhaven beer.

Where was I? Yes, fast running is most useful. Once when I was on a family holiday in some B&B flat in Hastings, I wandered off to do the town as teenagers do, but got lost. Eventually I found the right street, but all the Victorian houses looked the same and nearly all offered B&B. However, I knew ours had an aspidistra in a blue pot on the windowsill and there it was, so, somewhat relieved, I pushed open the heavy front door, charged up the three flights and into our flat. Horror upon horror, it was a different room with couple of men who seemed to be counting money at a table. For a nanosecond everybody froze; then they shouted:

'There's an intruder again,' and lunged towards me.

I ran down the stairs two at a time and out of the house. I could hear them coming so I just continued running and running until I was far away. Later, when I had recounted the accidental break-in to my parents, they kept asking why I didn't just explain but it was the evil look on their faces of the two men and my instinctive reaction to run that won the day.

Now France is steaming ahead – they can run too, it seems, even with all that weight, and make quick accurate passes, oh yes – a really solid try, converted too so they are ahead again. This, followed by a quick penalty, puts them even further ahead at 13-17. The two teams are really well matched, it could go either way.

Half a mile was my distance; cross-county running, as they called it then, was much too long and excruciatingly boring, so I sought relief by finding short-cuts across fields and meadows for myself and any like-minded pupils. Yes, we were still termed pupils rather than students (which was unfortunate for our boss-eyed headmaster, whom we used to unkindly joke could control neither types of pupils). I was king of the short-cuts for a time until it all went wrong. On this particular day I had reconnoitred an ingenious new short-cut near the beginning of a six-mile run and set off unobserved a little early. Nearly an hour later I was waiting back towards the end of the designated route in anticipation of re-joining my fellow pupils who had covered the full distance. I waited and waited for the goody-goody sporty mob to come by but they never appeared. It turned out the sports master had changed the route after I had left in some bloody-minded sense of fairness. As I finally returned, somewhat crestfallen, I was greeted by him and my supposedly loyal chums all slow-clapping me over the final few yards.

Oh, what a fantastic turnover, the French have it again but then hang onto the ball too long according to the ref. Another few minutes and it's half-time; hardly seems possible that 40 minutes have gone by already. Time for another beer.

After several incidents which I'd rather not go into, the school and my father felt it would be better for me and less stressful for them if I left after O-levels, so I was articled as an engineering apprentice and started work in a local company making electrical switchgear. How boring is that? And not even particularly local, as it transpired, five miles away actually, which I had to cycle every day. However, cycling is really just running but with a bicycle and while boring, it presented glorious opportunities for short-cuts.

The players are streaming back, all refreshed for the second half. No point-scoring action for a time but then out of the blue France earn another penalty, giving them a greater lead with 20 points. Just as it's not looking so good for England and their grand slam chances are fading, the French kindly commit some breach, giving England a penalty. This is painstakingly converted by Ferrell to make it 16-20, that's better. Now there's a scrum; surprisingly few in this game so far.

It's a good job I never had to join a scrum in my youth, I would have been eaten alive under that lot. Well, going to work, I found a short-cut which saved half a mile or so of my cycle route. It involved cutting through a large bus depot, down the side of the hundreds of red buses parked in long lines, through a big open shed and out onto the main road all at full speed. I'd been at it for several months until a totally inconsiderate driver left his bus too close and slightly tapered to the adjacent bus. My wide handlebars failed to quite make it through the gap and the bike became firmly wedged half way along. I tried to pull it out but was caught by two burly drivers.

'We've got him at last, Bob.'

'You training for the Tour de France, lad, or just on a bloody suicide mission?'

Okay, I thought, *it's a fair cop*, so I tried the sympathy ploy.

'I've got to ride five miles every day and then clock in

and they dock half an hour off my pay if I'm one minute late and…'

'You've scratched our buses, two buses at once indeed, I think we'll have to get the police down here.'

I panicked.

'Please don't do that, I'll be sacked from my apprenticeship and I've already been more or less expelled from school – I'll paint the marks out on Saturday and they won't show and I'll never come back.'

It's still 16-20 although Johnny May has just intercepted the ball from a poor French pass and is going like crazy. Crunch straight into an 18-stone French hulk, or should that be in kilograms in his case? Both a bit dazed but bravely carrying on.

Bob comes over all serious and menacing:

'You'll sure never come back here. If you do, we might crush you between these buses. We did it to the last lad, he ended up like the corned beef in a sandwich, so just bugger off and count yourself lucky.'

'Sorry,' I muttered meekly, 'but… ur… can I have my bike back?'

There's a few player change-overs now – gets a few fresh legs for the last eight minutes but surely there's a certain loss of momentum. England's charging forward, only five minutes to go. They need more than three points even if they extract a penalty, so there's not much chance. Then it's a TRY, great, no it's not quite down. The ref's studying pictures of Maro Itoje on the screen, there's a deathly hush, oh it must be surely. Yes, it's okay, great, fantastic, makes it 21-20. Another hush for Farrell as he takes his time, mechanically jerks his head and once again sends it straight between the posts. Brilliant, fantastic, but there's still a few minutes to go.

'Do you hear that, Bob, he wants his bike back too?'

They each silently walked to the cabs of the two buses and drove them a little way apart, so I grabbed my bike.

Free kick to France in the last two minutes but their final frantic push with players running everywhere is to no avail. England have won a resounding 23-20 victory. Redemption for England, disappointment for France and another Belhaven for me.

I put up my hand in thanks as I rode off, but Bob then shouted:

'Why don't you go to work on a bus? Safer for you and less damage for our busses.'

Buses are for wimps in the slow lane, I thought.

The Last Firework

IT HAPPENED NOT too far away, but I am obliged to disclose neither the village location nor the date except to say it was in the Scottish Highlands and the time was the early 2030s. I dare not be more precise because, if the details become common knowledge, the offending parties may be pursued under the regional government's new quest to prosecute more strongly historical cases involving infringement of their health and safety laws. Children were also involved in witnessing the offence so it would involve the most senior law courts in Scotland with their right to impose draconian sentences on crimes influencing those in their young and formative years. In fact, it might be best that you are discreet in admitting knowledge of this account, because its very possession might be deemed as harbouring seditious literature under our new compliance regulations.

On the November evening in question (possibly the fifth, but guidelines now disallow precise historical links with past acts of sabotage), darkness was descending and heavy dark clouds were gathering menacingly in the sky above. The villagers had wrapped themselves up against the cold evening chill and trudged the few hundred yards to the corner of Farmer MacKay's field. Some were old folk who could remember earlier in the century, when as young children they had clutched their parents' hands around a roaring bonfire and watched those terrifying fireworks burst into life. Long ago that had all been outlawed: firstly the fireworks were banned, then the bonfires with their fiery naked flames and lastly the effigy of a man named Guy Fawkes, now deemed a hero in Scotland. But in the Highlands old habits die hard and each year the villagers, as was their wont, had duly assembled in a silent vigil in the same field to defy the ban and release some illicit fireworks. Farmer MacKay was particularly supportive in allowing the corner of his field to be used. (Some cynics suggested it was the free pint of beer that each villager was expected to offer in return for this concession that fired his support.) This year, though, was to be the last, not owing to any move towards compliance among the villagers but simply because they only had one remaining firework.

The children were there too in their protective helmets, obediently clutching the hands of their government regulation guardians. At the appointed hour a person in a woollen pompom with a scarf concealing his face furtively produced from inside his anorak an ancient cylindrical firework on a stick. The yellow wrapping had mellowed and the edges of the cardboard cylinder were a little frayed. The man planted it on the hallowed ground where the bonfires had been, stood back and waited a moment as if in silent vigil to an event obliterated forever by over-zealous officialdom. He then ceremoniously lit it using a safety match which had been obtained on the antiques black market. It smouldered and flickered, and nothing happened. Folk sighed in resignation that even the remembrance gathering to mark the passing of another of their great celebrations of the past had been thwarted. Then, out of the silence, they heard a gentil hiss and suddenly the firework burst out, shooting up into the blackness where it exploded in an array of sparkling stars. For a moment of pure joy, it lit up the smiling faces of the delighted crowd.

As suddenly as the sky had erupted, it subsided into a hushed black silence. For a few moments the crowd just stood quietly in loyal respect of the sanctity their village secret inspired and the solemn pledge that no one would ever divulge the perpetrator. On occasions those from neighbouring areas thought they had seen a firework in the far distance, but these unsubstantiated reports were always met with incredulity and denial by the villagers.

It was the end of an era. The villagers sombrely filed back along the road towards the village. Even the children sensed the finality of the occasion and declined to run wildly around squabbling among themselves as they would normally in their restless hour before bedtime.

It was then that a miracle of circumstance occurred, as if nature was reminding them that not all was lost. The dark clouds above them parted a little to reveal through the gap a glorious eery light. The aurora borealis shone in all its glory: an amazing display of drifting yellow, green and blue hues that stopped the sombre gathering in its tracks. The villagers stood and peered up in sheer amazement and wonder that nature alone could outshine anything they had done and for a few brief minutes the heavens smiled upon them. Then the clouds folded back like the curtains of a show, and they returned to their homes, the children wearily to bed and the villagers with renewed warmth in their hearts to ponder the meaning of what had happened.

Circumstantial Evidence

POLLY PERKINS HAD established her little podiatry business in the Morningside area of Edinburgh soon after she graduated some ten years before. The premises had been a chiropodist's surgery for many years and when the owner retired and closed the business, she saw an opportunity to continue and perhaps extend the manicure side of the work. It had gone well, and she now employed a part-time receptionist who could deal with arrangements while she was out on home visits. These were necessary, as many of her clients were well-to-do elderly folk in the Victorian houses surrounding her practice.

It was late afternoon on the fateful day, and she was clearing up to go home. Her last client had long since gone and her receptionist had left to collect a child from school. As usual at this time of day, Polly was using the quiet time to tidy up. She had sterilised the instruments of her trade and had laid them out on the wee counter beside the reception area.

Suddenly a burly man in his late fifties bustled into the reception area. He paused and seemed somewhat ill at ease before asking:

'Would you be able to attend to Mrs Henderson's toenails? You've done them before, I believe. She lives just nearby, in 7 Aprilla Court.'

Polly was well acquainted with Mrs Henderson: she was the most ancient and reclusive of Polly's older clients and lived a frugal existence among the cobwebs of her oak-panelled rooms – indeed, Polly's receptionist referred to her as Miss Havisham. Polly suspected her occasional visits were to lend a sympathetic ear to Mrs Henderson's whining monologue about the state of the modern world more than concern for her corns and toenails. But Polly kindly went along with this and each time spent extra time chatting to her amicably, deeming it the price one pays to have such affluent clients. In any case, Mrs Henderson always paid promptly, albeit with no gratuity. But why was this man acting for her?

'It could not be before next week, Mr…'

'Mr Smith,' he said, adding by way of explanation, 'I help look after her from time to time as I'm a good friend of her son. I'm really afraid that timing would not do – I was hoping you could do this today; you see, it's urgent as she's very ill.'

Polly was taken aback. Mrs Henderson had mentioned a long-lost son in the Middle East whom, after they fell out, she had not seen for many years; but nobody that looked after her. She was about to decline when he added:

'I know it's inconvenient but I would pay you, say, £150 cash just to do her toenails.'

At that he opened his wallet to show that it contained plenty of notes. She noticed he wore black leather gloves although it was not particularly cold. Perhaps he wore gloves for style although he certainly did not appear stylish in any way; indeed, slightly dishevelled and possibly Mediterranean, now she came to notice.

Well, she was only going to go straight home tonight and the £150 was very tempting, so after a moment she said:

'Since she's been a good client of mine for so long, I'll make an exception and go round there after I've cleared up here. I'll need to repack my home-visit bag and collect these instruments too.'

She went into the back surgery to collect her bag while he waited in the reception area. On returning to the counter a couple of minutes later to collect the items lying there, she noticed her largest toe scalpel, the one she used to clear out the hard crud under the big toe, was missing. She looked around and even peered under the counter, but it was just not there, and she was a little flustered under his gaze. Perhaps she was misremembering or had mislaid it somewhere else; no matter, she had others. She was nearly ready to go but he went to the entrance door, saying:

'I'll leave you to it and walk on to Aprilla Court ahead of you in order to ensure she's ready for your visit. Could I see you there in about an hour?'

Aprilla Court was only a short walk away, so she took her time shutting up the shop and one hour later duly arrived at 7 Aprilla Court. She rang the doorbell, but it was quite some time before Mr Smith opened up and she had begun to wonder whether this was some elaborate hoax. Eventually he opened the door, still wearing his black gloves. He looked particularly sombre and somewhat flustered. After a pause he said hesitantly:

'I'm very sorry but I'm afraid Mrs Henderson died while I was away seeing you. It was her request that I see you; she was quite adamant about it, although she was so ill.' He paused and then added, 'But I would still like you to cut her toenails if you can manage it, being her last wish and all that.'

Polly responded sharply:

'I'm very sorry, you must have had a shock but I'm a podiatrist, Mr Smith, not a mortician.' Then she felt that was rather cold and inappropriate in the circumstances and added, 'But I suppose I could.'

Mrs Henderson was in bed and Mr Smith had draped the eiderdown right across her so that only her feet were visible out of the end. Polly unintentionally shivered but then braced herself to carry on and quickly set to with her implements, fighting off an impulse to flee the house as she clipped away at the lifeless toes. There was no point in fussing too much and she declined to file them smooth. After a few moments, she gathered up the towel on which the clippings had fallen and having nowhere to put it, folded it neatly into her bag. He duly handed over the £150 and she offered her condolences, adding:

'Will you be informing her son in Dubai immediately? He should be informed even if, as I understand, he has not seen her for a long time.'

'Yes, I will contact him this evening. Thank you for agreeing to come round.'

She still felt uncomfortable about it all but having nothing further to add, she left, leaving him there still wearing those leather gloves.

Later at home, sipping a stiff gin and tonic, she started to reflect on the oddity of the situation. Who was this Mr Smith anyway? Why had she not met him before if he was a friend of her estranged son, and why was he suddenly so attentive to Mrs Henderson? She did not sleep well that night.

It was about coffee time the next morning; Polly was already on her second cup and still feeling tired. She had seen her first client and the next was not due for twenty minutes or so. It was then that two police officers entered her little surgery and asked her to close up and accompany them to the police station to answer some questions. Momentarily she was completely taken aback but reasoned they just wanted her version of the odd events concerning Mrs Henderson the previous day; presumably there would be a postmortem and such like. Why it had to be at the police station she didn't know, but she postponed her immediate appointments and followed them out to the police car.

Later in the interview room she recounted the events exactly as they had occurred. They recorded all she said and listened intently but at no point asked her for any elaboration. By the end she felt them looking at her in a distinctly incredulous fashion. The more senior of the two then leaned forward and, picking his words carefully said:

'Miss Perkins, before we continue this interview, we are obliged to caution you and advise you to seek legal support.'

The second officer then explained:

'For your information, we were informed late last night by an unknown caller of cries for help from 7 Aprilla Court. We gained access and found that a Mrs Henderson of that address had been murdered in her bed. The assumed murder weapon was a podiatrist's scalpel covered in blood which had been plunged into the victim's heart. The scalpel is currently being examined for fingerprints. Also, since you've been here at the station, we have retrieved some toenail clippings from a towel in your podiatrist's bag for DNA comparison with that of the victim.'

Polly was horrified and blurted out in panic:

'But you've gained totally the wrong end of the stick. Why on earth would I want to harm her? She was a good client of mine.'

'Because,' he said coldly, 'this morning we checked with her solicitor and he tells us that, along with her son whom we have so far been unable to trace, you are an equal beneficiary of her will.'

Polly looked totally aghast and turned ice white in shock. The senior officer said:

'We believe you paid her a visit to attend to her feet when she was unwell and knowing she was leaving you half her wealth, saw an opportunity and took it. You were no doubt hoping later to blame this, er… mystery visitor for her murder, but so far we have found no finger prints belonging to such a person.'

'But he must have been her son or a friend of her son's who did this to get all of the inheritance,' she blurted out.

The police officer looked at her unflinchingly and added:

'But you admitted you cut her toenails after she was dead. Was that not to explain why you were there?'

Before Polly could respond, he added:

'Surely you don't expect us to believe you cut the nails of a dead client merely at the behest of some stranger.'

Village Kirk Hall

I RECENTLY CAME across a most elegant village hall. While admiring it, a man playing football with two young children in the garden of the house next door came across. On greeting him I asked,

'How does such a small village come to have such a modern and beautiful hall?'

'It's due to our wedding,' he responded.

For a minute I thought he was going to stop there but then he elaborated with this story.

'About ten years ago there was a wee stooshie in the village. For over 100 years the Kirk Session had let out their kirk hall to the village as needed. Then the Church of Scotland decided to start closing rural kirks, like the Beeching cuts to branch railways in the 1960s. The Village Association, who thought of it as their hall, arranged for a local lawyer to place a pre-emptive bid for the hall under the right-to-buy scheme. Also, the rich developer in the house next door saw it as a golden opportunity to expand his premises and placed a bid. For several months the Association, the Kirk and the rich developer scandalised one and other and truth was thin on the ground.

'It was at this time that I finally made an honest lass of the lovely Linda and asked her to marry me. The wedding arrangements were that after the service we would go to the kirk hall and have coffee provided by a church lady, then make our way to the Cock and Bull where the proprietor would provide a full reception complete with romantic songs by Jim Reeves to please my new mother-in-law. What could go wrong?

'Well, everything. It was first noticed by the district ranger who was walking by with his dog towards the end of the service. He saw a distinct orange glow at the hall windows, so he peered inside. It was already a furnace. The wooded kitchen units had disintegrated and the window-panes were too hot to touch. The ranger fumbled with his mobile, but there was no reception, so he panicked and ran into the church shouting that the village hall was on fire. Eventually the fire engines arrived, having been delayed because their satnav showed a kirk hall but not a village hall.

'Once the excitement had waned, the proprietor of the Cock and Bull invited us all and we had a most enjoyable afternoon and evening. Petty bickering about the kirk or village hall seemed rather out of place when it had burnt down, so the subject was put on hold. A week later, both the Session and the Association decided to meet and plan a new hall and, since there was nowhere else, they met in the back room of the pub. They assumed tea would be served, but since the proprietor appeared with wine and plenty of glasses on the house it would have been churlish not to accept. They agreed there should be another one the next month and the one after that.

'It was after three months that the rich developer made a substantial offer to the Kirk Session for the hall, as it was all ruined, with a proviso that the Kirk must use all the money to build a new hall. They were stunned; had he had a Pauline conversation, or was he ensuring the hall would not be built next to him? The insurance company quickly recommended acceptance and over the next year they finished the plans for Village Kirk Hall, as they agreed to call it. Within two years it was built and it even won a design award a few weeks ago.'

The children were becoming restless so I said,

'Then it all ended happily in the end?'

'Absolutely,' he said. 'The Village Association and the Kirk are happy, the owner of the Cock and Bull is happy, the insurance company is happy and the church lady, who had switched on the old coffee urn without adding water that morning, is happy because she believes she was instrumental in God's plan.'

'And what about yourselves?'

'Oh, we're happy too. Each year the village celebrates our wedding anniversary with a firework display.'

University Cuts

MIKE MCKENZIE WAS a first-year student at a university in Edinburgh. He had heard that Freshers' Week was fun but following the COVID-19 pandemic of the early '20s it had never recovered its coveted place in student life. He was not particularly sporty and most of the clubs failed to attract him except for the cycle club. It was thus one sunny evening a few months later that Mike found himself in a bar in Rose Street where they had decided to meet before they set off on an evening cycle ride. He settled down with a Coca-Cola next to Lucy who was a mad keen cyclist; they would all return later after the ride for something stronger. He had had a long day with an exam in the afternoon and felt really tired.

A little later he was endeavouring to keep up with other club members cycling along Princes Street.

'Wait for me,' he called out as they nudged the 20mph speed limit.

The others all had posh bikes with 21 derailleur gears while he had to make do with one of the loan bikes supplied by the university. Indeed, owing to the severe university cuts they had reduced the number of wheels on the loan bikes from two to one. It was recognised that they required more skill to ride and the authorities had offered free training courses to students who had difficulty balancing on a single-wheeled bike (SWB). However, students, being very agile, soon mastered the art and could ride them at reasonable speeds.

The proliferation of SWBs across the city had led to criticism from motoring organisations who said they should be used on the designated paths and the pavements. The SWB folk responded that they had a right to use the roads and that in any case the motorists were often using the pavements for parking. The University, having the student interest to the forefront, established jointly with Edinburgh Council an SWB Committee to examine the matter. The Committee consisted of senior professors from the statistics department (as part of their deployment following the demise of COVID-19) and two councillors. After much research this Committee unearthed a Ruling (Hampshire Constabulary, Shanklin, TMO Bartlett, 7/11/2000) made by the Constabulary of Hampshire regarding a case of a single-wheeled bike on the Isle of Wight. This ruling argued that under the Highways Act, Section 72 (1835), such vehicles should be used on the road and not the pavement.

Mike was thus legally pedalling along the centre of Princes Street that evening, albeit lagging well behind his compatriots, but two things were worrying him. It was getting dark, and front and back lights were mandatory after sunset as per the Ruling. The issue was where to put them, as there was only him above the saddle level. However, he had fitted a forward-facing inspection lamp to his crash helmet and strapped a torch with red cellophane over it on his back. The other thing was the absence of brakes. Although not engineers, even the professors of statistics and the councillors had realised that application of brakes on an SWB would simply rotate the rider abruptly downwards by 90 degrees and potentially smash his front lamp. Fortunately, on further perusal of the original Act of 1835, they discovered that it excluded fixed-drive vehicles from the requirement for brakes; and the SWB was most certainly a fixed-drive vehicle.

Edinburgh Council, for their part, made SWBs readily available for loan all over the city by storing them in their conveniently named Re-Cycle Bins. The university, as their contribution, encouraged all students to make use of this facility and, as a mark of university approval, designated that they should henceforth be called Uni-cycles. It could have ended happily there, but the university was on a cost-cutting roll, having reduced student transport from four wheels to two wheels to one wheel, and saw no reason to stop there. Indeed, zero wheels is essentially a stick and the pogo stick, with its jumping spring, had been a favourite in former times when most of the committee had been in their youth. Also, they argued, the sticks would be easier to store in the Re-Cycle Bins. However, the Principal eventually put a stop to this line of progression on the basis that it was jumping ahead.

Meanwhile, Mike had reached the Scott Monument, but unfortunately his single wheel had become entrapped in one of the tramlines so he had to keep travelling along, wherever it went. A tram was coming along behind him so he just had to keep going, but it was catching him up very quickly. Would he reach the end of the line at York Place in time? Faster and faster he rode, but the tram was soon right on top of him. He felt it slam into his wheel; his head crashed down to the hard ground with a bang and all went blank.

He raised his head slowly from the table. There was a pint of Belhaven in front of him and opposite sat Lucy looking somewhat coy. He blinked and rubbed his eyes, gazing questioningly at her.

'They left half an hour ago, so now you're left with me.'

Realisation began to dawn.

'They could have woken me.'

'You were obviously tired after your exam and you looked so peaceful, I suggested they left you to sleep it off,' she smiled. 'And then I thought you would want a drink when you came to. Mind you, I did not expect you to fall forward onto the table like that.'

Mike was still rubbing his head.

'And while you were dozing, I was reading this leaflet. The Uni wants suggestions from students on saving costs and they'll pay if implemented. I thought of suggesting they sack some of the more useless staff for starters.'

Well, I might have some other ideas,' said Mike, 'but meanwhile, let me treat you to a drink while I explain.'

Bulb of Percussion

BOOKS OFTEN TELL a story between their covers, but some tell a story by their very possession. Such is the case for a book I have had many years, collecting dust on my shelves, a book awarded to me as the first-year history prize at a school assembly. I was amazed to receive it because my academic performance in all school subjects ranged from poor to unremarkable and this included history, the most boring subject of all. However, it was awarded under somewhat strange circumstances.

My family lived for a short time at Midhurst in Sussex when I was about eleven years old. I found school very boring and, much of the time, family life even more so. One Saturday morning near the end of the long summer break when I was probably being really tiresome, my father gave me an Ordnance Survey map and said in so many words, on your bike. So this I did and found I really enjoyed cycling around the local lanes exploring small villages at the foot of the South Downs. They had interesting names such as Didling, with its and flint walls, Cocking, which had a chalk pit full of fossils, and Heyshott, where you could get tangerine ice lollies. I noticed on the map, printed in antique script, that there were many tumuli in the area. I read up about them and managed to locate a few. I was intrigued that the bones of buried stone-age folk were probably still within the grassy mounds that I had discovered.

On one of these forays, near the village of Upper

Norwood I believe, I found more than expected when I located a particularly prominent tumulus. It was being excavated by an 'old' lady (probably about 50, looking back), who seemed rather unkempt and was scraping away at a part of the tumulus she had dug into near the base of the mound. She explained she was a volunteer resident archaeologist employed by the county and had been asked to make preliminary searches of local late stone age and early bronze age tumuli. I was totally intrigued and asked if I could help.

'Well, I suppose you can't do much harm.'

Her slight reluctance washed over me as I immediately set to work with enthusiasm. She taught me to scrape carefully with a funny little trowel in case I disturbed anything significant. I continued for many hours, occasionally punctuated by tea provided from her stained flask and the cheese sandwiches I had grabbed on leaving the house. By late afternoon I felt I should return home but there was obviously a lot more scaping needed.

'Can I come again tomorrow to finish this part?'

'Yes, I suppose so, but you should ask your parents if they are happy about it.'

On the way down the chalky track, I noticed an old caravan and realised that was where she stayed.

I explained my adventure to my mum and said I wanted to go back the next day and how I might even discover a skeleton – well, you had to make it seem purposeful for adults who had no lure of the ancient. She promised to discuss it with my father. He later asked a load of dumb questions about who this woman was but he didn't stop me going off the next morning. In fact, I went on scraping and digging with the old archaeologist for the best part of a week until we hit gold.

Well, not gold but flint, to be precise. Everybody knows

that there is lots of flint within the chalk on the South Downs – indeed, half the old houses seem to be built of it – but this was not any old flint occurring there by nature. It was very special pieces of flint that had the bulb of percussion on their surfaces. She explained that, when flint is struck with a hammer or, in the case of a stone age man, with a boulder or even another piece of flint, the vibration of the impact causes the flint to fracture in a bulb shape with odd ripples on the surface. These are like the ridges around the shell of a mollusc and signify the surface of man-worked flint tools. Similar percussion waves are formed if a piece of solid tar is struck with a hammer. To me the bulb of percussion sanctified the flint: it had been formed by a human being thousands of years ago and now I could touch it too, running my grubby fingers over the characteristic ripples, bridging the divide in time between him and me.

Once discovered I scraped with renewed enthusiasm. Having the sharp eyes and focused attention of the young once they are fired up, I found lots of flint implements, broken arrowheads and skin scrapers that would have been buried with the warrior in the tumulus. Edie – she had now divulged her name – then said:

'We must now stop and fill it in.'

I looked at her with amazement.

'But we must go on to find the bones and things, after all this work.'

'No. We have now proved this to be a burial mound and can date it from the flint tools we have found. There is no need to disturb the dead. That's not the purpose.'

I was totally crestfallen. I had nursed a vision, if not of peer approval from my school chums, then at least some understanding by them if I had actually found a body. They would never understand why I had been digging with an old archaeologist named Edie on the South Downs for the last week of my holiday and then simply helped her fill it in. Indeed, I'm not sure I fully understood myself at the time.

She did, though, take me back to the caravan and we sat outside in the sun drinking tea and eating some cakes she had found. Then she said, as I was about to leave:

'Look, all these flint tools have to be recorded and sent to the County Museum in Chichester where the best from here and elsewhere may go into a glass case, but most will be stored forever in cardboard boxes. If a couple of pieces were to go missing...' She slid a nice flint scraper and a broken arrowhead in my direction – '... say for many years, I'm sure the ongoing advance of archaeology would not be seriously damaged.'

I slipped them in my pocket next to my dirty handkerchief and waved Edie goodbye as I rode off down the track.

I never saw her again, but I think she must have told someone at my school about the assistance she had received. I have little evidence for this but when the prize of the book with its carefully inscribed frontispiece was awarded, I remember going up to the stage a little cautiously as I thought they must have the wrong name. The history teacher handing out the prize glanced at me with a knowing grin and emphasised to the assembly that this year it was awarded for the history of the stone age.

Family Tradition

ON A WEE island off the West Coast of Scotland, there was a growing concern among its few inhabitants. Fish and farm food they had aplenty, but the proposed increases in electricity cost would be devastating. In times past they had relied on the MacGregor family, the island's electricians, to see them through, but they were not sure the current young Sparky MacGregor was up to the job.

In the 1950s, Sparky's grandfather had wired up their cottages to the new lampposts to power their 40-watt bulbs and Bakelite radios. In the 1980s, his father had connected their cottages by underground cable to the one and only substantial mansion on the island, owned by an absentee landlord. The landlord had found his frost protection costs were the highest in the west. Now it was up to the current Sparky to find a solution for the villagers to the staggering price rises.

The responsibility lay heavily upon him one evening as he joined the community leaders assembled in the back room of the Ship Inn. The opportunities afforded to his forebears seemed unlikely in these days of electric cars and smart meters. Old Ted, who was already three sheets to the wind, suddenly announced:

'I'm told that the government's new car charging point by the village hall offers free electricity. The Scottish government has made it free to encourage these new-fangled electric cars.'

There was one of those hushed silences that can occur

in crowded spaces for no particular reason, and the word 'free' hung in the air like holy incense.

'We don't have any electric cars,' someone objected, but Sparky wasn't listening.

A thought had been seeded, which he enthusiastically developed over the following weeks. Four damaged electric cars, which were still intact but had been written off as 'uneconomic to repair' by an insurance company, were purchased at scrap value. There were four small groups of cottages on the island and Sparky established what he called a 'discharging point' near each group where the stored power in the cars could be fed to the direct-current resistive heaters in the cottages. It involved much technical calculation and clandestine underground wiring, but he was on a mission and worked hard at it every night.

And so it came to be, a few months later, that each of the four electric cars, on a daily rota basis, would absorb about 100kWh of free energy from the island's charging point and be driven the short distance to its allocated cottage group. There it would be plugged in to dispense its 100kWh of energy as heat to the cottages as required. The normal 240-volt mains were of course retained to maintain a modicum of normal lighting and low-power usage for appearances' sake.

The increase in charging point usage was noticed by the authorities, but the islanders claimed it was English tourists. Several times Argyll and Bute Council sent officials out to investigate, but each time the wee ferry across to the island broke down (owing to, believe it or not, electrical faults in the engine that Sparky had to repair). They eventually gave up. At the Kirk services, the minister prayed that the government would continue its encouragement of electric vehicles. Sparky was rewarded by being elected chairman of the Village Association.

In fact, it was a good ending all round. The islanders were happy with their fuel costs, the Council was happy that their policy on electric vehicles for the islands was exonerated, the insurance company was happy to offload their crashed cars, the landlord of the Ship Inn was happy they were meeting there, the minister was happy to have his prayers answered and Sparky was happy that his family's honour was maintained.

Indeed, his 12-year-old son was already working on a scheme to fit current transformer coils around the cables ahead of the smart meters. He got the idea from his dad's electric toothbrush which lay in the bathroom. It was charged from the magnetism of the alternating current in the charging base and had no electric contact with the holder.

As a true MacGregor, he'd already realised that it's better to outsmart the authorities than argue with them.

Final Curtain

BABY BOBBY LOLLED back in his highchair and pushed the remaining soggy bread around the white plastic tray with his forefinger. They had tried to feed him and occasionally the spoon had reached his mouth but more often than not the soggy bread had landed in a sickly mess on his knitted woollen cardigan. Quite a lot had found its way to the stock of encrusted food from other meals on the curtains next to his chair. Some of them looked very cross.

Anyway, who were these people? His mum seemed to leave him with them most days and all they did was to sit him down in front of a large black and white TV screen and expect him to do nothing. Then, just as he was getting tired and prepared to do nothing, they would start exercises and bounce a big balloon towards him or ask him to throw a fluffy ball. If he escaped from his chair to investigate the surroundings, he was collared before he got too far and determinedly returned to his seat. When his mum came to collect him, they seemed to be all smiling and friendly as if he had enjoyed the day.

Then the two-year-old Bobby grew up to be 22 years old, by which time he had a job, a partner and a baby daughter named Cathy. And then from 22 years to 42 years, by which time his partner had left and he looked after Cathy alone. Then from 42 to 62, when he retired early and played excellent golf and from 62 to 82, after which he played increasingly poor golf. Then from 82 to some age he could not remember because his memory was fading, they put him in a home where they felt he would benefit from institutional care for the elderly.

Old Bobby lolled back in his chair and pushed the remaining soggy mince around the plain white plate balanced on his lap cushion. He had managed to feed himself but it was not a good day for his arthritis and some of it had landed in a sticky mess on his knitted cardigan. Quite a lot had found its way to the stock of encrusted food from other meals on the curtains next to his chair. Some of them looked very cross

Anyway, who were these people? Cathy had abandoned him to them but all they did was to seat him down in the conservatory with a large TV screen and expect him to do nothing. Then, just as he was getting tired and prepared to do nothing, they would start exercises and throw a balloon in his direction or ask him to hold a ball. If he extracted himself from his chair to investigate his surroundings, they would collar him before he got too far, in case he had a fall they said, and return him to his seat.

In moments of insight, he resigned himself to the thought that life is simply a sandwich with anything of interest layered between two plain white slices of well-intentioned but restrictive care. Surely there must be more to life than that before the final curtain was drawn; something to fire him up once more.

Inexplicitly, that was exactly what happened. His pal two chairs along had caused it by insisting on the right to smoke his pipe.

'I've smoked since I was 15,' he would boast to the young care worker as she once again wheeled him from the garden lean-to shelter back into the conservatory, 'and it never did me no harm.'

Never a truer word spoken, she thought to herself, but said nothing and hurried off to attend duties elsewhere.

On the fateful day he had tucked his pipe in his jacket pocket when wheeled back into his place in the conservatory and it had quietly smouldered away while he napped. His jacket was well alight by the time Bobby noticed it and he jumped up surprisingly quickly and started banging a cushion against his pal's side but it just fanned the flames and made things worse. Then the curtains burst into flames – weren't they meant to be incombustible; maybe not when encrusted with food. His pal seemed to have given up or fainted and was just slumped back in the chair. The little lady who sat opposite and never spoke came over and the two of them managed to drag his pal out of the chair by his legs. His body went down with a bang onto the floor and the little lady shouted:

'Quickly, wrap him in the rug, it'll stifle the fire in his jacket.'

Together they rolled him up in the old Indian rug as best they could just as two of the staff arrived. One of them bravely managed to yank down the whole curtain array and run to the exit door, dragging them into the garden. The other carer was desperately trying to work out how to start a fire extinguisher she'd found while at the same time ringing for the emergency services on her mobile.

Three hours later the firemen had left, and Bobby's pal was tucked up in hospital having been diagnosed with a minor stroke but mercifully sustaining only superficial burns. The poor staff who had saved the day were being questioned on their lack of attention to duty in allowing him to smoke at all. The blackened conservatory, soaked with water from the firemen's hoses, was declared out of bounds for the foreseeable future.

Bobby and the little lady, whom he now noticed had

particularly twinkly eyes, had been treated for minor scuffs and grazes following their haste to roll up the rug. They had also been treated by the matron to an unscheduled coffee and cake and were chatting in an animated fashion to each other about other emergencies they had each experienced in times past.

On her next visit Cathy was amazed to be met at the door by her father who seemed to have regained his spirit. He even introduced her to some of the other residents. She observed the fire-damaged conservatory, normally partially concealed behind an old curtain, but he just said something odd about how the final curtain could not be drawn yet as it had been burnt down.